THE MAPMAKER

The Mapmaker

A Novel of Ancient Greece

COURT ATCHINSON

Court Atchinson

FOR VIVIAN,

without whom my skull

is an empty cup.

Contents

Acknowledgments and Sources

In equal parts homage and shameless piracy, I have borrowed "winedark sea" and a handful of other phrases from Homer and Virgil. The histories of Herodotus figure prominently throughout, especially as to the Scythians, whose culture has been further augmented by modern archaeological sources. Plutarch's *Parallel Lives* contains the best biography of that colorful cad, Alcibiades. Thucydides is the primary source on the Peloponnesian Wars (and Plato's inspiration for "Atlantis"). Materials on Socrates and Plato are plentiful in histories ancient and modern, but I found I.F. Stone's *The Trial Of Socrates*, Will Durant's *The Life Of Greece* and Carl J. Richard's *Twelve Greeks And Romans Who Changed The World* particularly helpful for this narrative.

The "Think, Lady Moon" fragment is from *The Idylls* of Theocritus; *Daphnis And Chloe* by Longus provides descriptions of Lesbos. On some matters concerning the Greek deities, I consulted Hesiod's *Theogeny*, but my primary guide to things mythological, including the very real Dactylists, was Robert Graves's indispensable *The Greek Myths*.

The sixteenth century Peruvian rebel, Juan Barragan, left an extraordinary memoir about the assassination of Francisco Pizarro, which I have adapted to my own purposes, and one character herein quotes a lyric from *Tenderness Junction*, a 1967 album by The Fugs.

Personal thanks are owed to Cheri Ezzell, George Davis and Becky Anderson, Melody and Sylvan Reynolds and Martin Shupack (who also played Polyxo to my Kasperius) for their helpful readings and encouragement.

Along with many useful suggestions, my good friend, award-winning poet David Thomson, PhD, contributed something of which I myself am utterly incapable: poetry. He provided a sumptuous buffet of verse from which I constructed the oracular rhymes of the sibyls, without which this work would have been impossible.

And finally, there is boundless gratitude to my best friend, critic, proofreader, booster, fan, agent and smart device, the light of my life and fire of my loins, my wife Vivian.

Two Historical Quotes

The importance of maps in the campaigns of Alexander the Great is a matter which has never been fully resolved. Most writers have supposed that Alexander relied at first upon the geography obtained by his father, Philip, during that king's sorties in Asia Minor, and that after reaching Persepolis had information from the conquered tribes to guide him farther East. But Eratosthenes, in his *On the Measurement of the Earth*, writes that Alexander carried with him "diverse charts," among which he principally consulted that of an obscure Mytilenean cartographer, Timalcus the Lesbian. This map, the only known presently existing copy of which is to be found in the Ptolemaic Library in Alexandria, is said to have been drawn a few decades before Alexander's time and to have shown many wonders not found on other maps of its day.

Skylos of Kalampoki
Historium hellenika,
Book 12, Part II

What Plato recognized, therefore, is that the study of geography fell neither within the realm of science, nor of art, but was properly a branch of philosophy. For this assertion we have no less an expert witness than Diogenes the Cynic, who tells us that, upon opening his Academy in 387 B.C., Plato had engraved upon the facade the words: "That no one enter here who is not a geographer."

Rousseau
Discours sur les sciences
et les arts, 1750

Maps

Chapter One

Lesbos

WITH LOVE AND A CROW, that's how my troubles began. Ask anyone if that isn't a terrible combination, a conflux of signs tumid with threat. A fool could read in it the pulse of fate's current, the sea from which no vessel is delivered nor any man saved. A fool could have seen; I could not, and in the arrogance of youth would have ignored it anyway.

Love's name was Melisanthe, Sappho's own "sweet honey'd bloom," a cradle name whose promise of amber delight was already ripely kept in that spring of our giddy adolescence. I heeded not the adage that uncured honey drives men mad.

The murdered crow kept his name well hid, but I know whose malignant envoy he was, what black and bitter god he served, though now, in this more quiet season of my passage, I no longer fear him, nor his progeny, nor their ilk, nor their cruel and pointless jests, nor their black mouths hungry for our tears. Now, only memory and ghosts populate the ambit of my crossings.

Think, Lady Moon, how my love came to be.
Turn, Magic Wheel, and drive my lover home.

It was the last sweet season of our youth. One moment Melisanthe was my playmate; in the next, her scent, the pert swell of her haunches, those remarkable eyes, stirred in me a sudden, intoxicated passion wholly new and unexpected. She was a storm to scatter my wits and I was quickly lost to that delirious farce called "first love." In that state I was no doubt as richly comic as any who'd ever played the role, and worse, an unlikely suitor to such beauty - an awkward, bookish boy, an indifferent athlete among young Olympians. I had these traits from my father.

A linguist and scholar, Father was a gentle, dreamy man who neither flogged nor fornicated with our slaves as is widely held permissible. At times he was so lost in thought he failed to recognize his own children in the street. He knew every-thing, I believed, and noticed nothing, least of all the affairs of his family.

But when I showed interest in his work, he began, with casual absent-mindedness, to lead me from the aleph-bet of Phoenician, mother to our own Greek, through the oxen track of Boustrephedon, the newer Ionian script and, of course, the archaic Aeolic dialect of Sappho.

I went on to master the ornate swirls of Persian, the birds-foot scratches of cuneiform, the boxy symmetry of Aramaic. My father's vast, untidy library lay open before me. I plunged into his books and scrolls of papyrus, vellum and leather, his tablets of copper and clay, happily browsing, lost in the dreams of a dozen dusty tongues. Of Homer and Hesiod I drank deeply; in Zeno and Pindar I feasted. Side by side with the latest plays from Athens I read rare, exotic fragments of the K'Habiru epic and the bloodsongs of Pnum-Veda. Father and I even amused ourselves with the clumsy Latin imitations of Homer, though nothing of value, he said, could ever come from such a barbarous tribe.

Nor was geography neglected. I tagged along when he addressed a symposium in Sardis. There, among that splendid city's many treasures, we saw a replica of Herodotus's bronze map of the world, from which I could scarcely be dragged away. Back in Mytilene, Father suggested I try my own hand at it, a project I undertook so avidly that I often fell asleep over my work and woke the next day with the inky contour of Libya or Thrace upon my cheek.

The intellectual life is much prized in Greece, but in moderation only. Aeschylus, after all, was prouder of having fought the Persians than of writing the *Oresteia*. A playwright might box or wrestle, a citharode stitch rhyme above his lyre one day, then take up axe and shield the next. Of this Hellenic ideal of manhood I was sorely lacking. In short, I was much in danger of becoming my father. Yet to everyone's surprise, Melisanthe returned my affection, perhaps because she was, in her own way, different, too.

To her mother's despair, Melisanthe had not at the expected age withdrawn indoors to practice womanly arts and cultivate a fashionable pallor. When we boys and girls were separated at age six, she ran crying to join us, and given a choice, preferred our company still. She would Artemis be, she said, not pale Aphrodite. Her limbs were tawny from the sun, in play she was more coltish than dainty and her laugh was as unbridled as a child's.

But it was her eyes that astonished. Most Greeks have dark eyes: Melisanthe's seemed to have sprung directly from the sea, a pure and dazzling emerald. In their crystal depths I tossed, helpless as foam upon the tide.

Whatever the reason, when lessons were done it was I with whom Melisanthe retired to some shady nook. It was I who sang Homer and the nine books of Sappho to her. It was I, favored of the gods, who laid figs and honeycakes to her insatiable lips, a mouth, she insisted, too sticky with baklava crumbs for me to kiss. And it was I, happy beyond measure yet miserably uncertain, who listened to her maddening chatter, for she spoke not a syllable but was couched in riddling gibber. When she was not teasingly enigmatic, she was whimsical as a cricket. She would not say she loved me, not in so many words, and of course I could not ask; on the subject of most importance to me she spoke, if at all, with breezy nonchalance. But no matter. At the end of the day it was upon my tingling thigh, and no one else's, that she lay her wondrous head, one plump arm flung carelessly across my leg. The happy, excruciating summer lay endlessly before us. Another rhyme, another honey'd fig.

Just so we lounged one perfect morning. Melisanthe rose with a lazy stretch.

I almost forgot to tell you, she said, and I girded myself for some fresh nonsense. The isle of Melos, she said. My aunt lives there. Mother thinks I'll be safer if war comes. I leave at noontide. Until autumn, perhaps.

This time she wasn't kidding. My face must have looked as hideously contorted as my brain felt.

Come, Timalcus, don't sulk. It's only for the summer.

She kissed me then, full on the mouth, for the first time. What memory demands, memory will provide - the kiss must then be recalled as warm, sweet, sticky, wet, tender. But if I were to be honest, I think I was so numb I scarcely felt it. And just like that, she was gone. That was Melisanthe, all over, a careless girl.

I found myself in a state of stupefied anguish and without clear memory of going there, at the harbor of Mytilene, where the little merchant shallop that would carry my love to Melos made ready to sail. Unable to bear the sight, I turned away and dragged my feet along the strand. Bitterness choked my heart. Melisanthe was leaving me; she would find someone new to love. So black and paralyzed was my mind that I could not concentrate. I thought of suicide. I was unmanned.

That's when I met the crow.

He began immediately to mock me, landing just ahead along the lapping shoals, spreading his huge wings, taunting me with his croak, tirelessly repeating this insolent burlesque.

I screamed at him to no effect. When I ran at him he flapped lazily away and settled again beyond my grasp, his sharp *"cak!"* a derisive mimicry of my own shrill voice.

I picked up a stone.

Malicious jokester, I panted, ridicule my grief no more! Leave me, in sweet Aphrodite's name, to die in peace!

It was the invocation of Cypris that did it, of course. My usual clumsy, girlish skill in throwing vanished; the cursed missile sped like divine lightning from my fist, smashing the beast's brain as he rose cackling from the sand.

I ran to him, whooping, and stood over his corpse, beating my breast. Die, make an end of it, Hektor! I cried. Dogs and kites will have you, every scrap!

Slowly my senses returned. My Achillean jubilation gave way to the rising dread of blood-guilt unexpunged. I had committed a terrible crime against the ancient crow god, and in panic I thought to conceal the evidence. Better to rip my tongue from its hinges than confess this deed, but it was already too late. I had been seen, that much was certain; Cronus was watching, and he had witnessed the murder of his child.

The crow was heavy and still warm. Wading into the shallows, I flung his carcass against the sea, but the stubborn waves, despite a clearly retreating tide, spat the monster back. Poseidon refused all complicity in my act, and I can't say I blame him.

I took the ghastly thing, sea-sodden and ponderous with shame, into the dunes, where I scooped a shallow grave and covered it over.

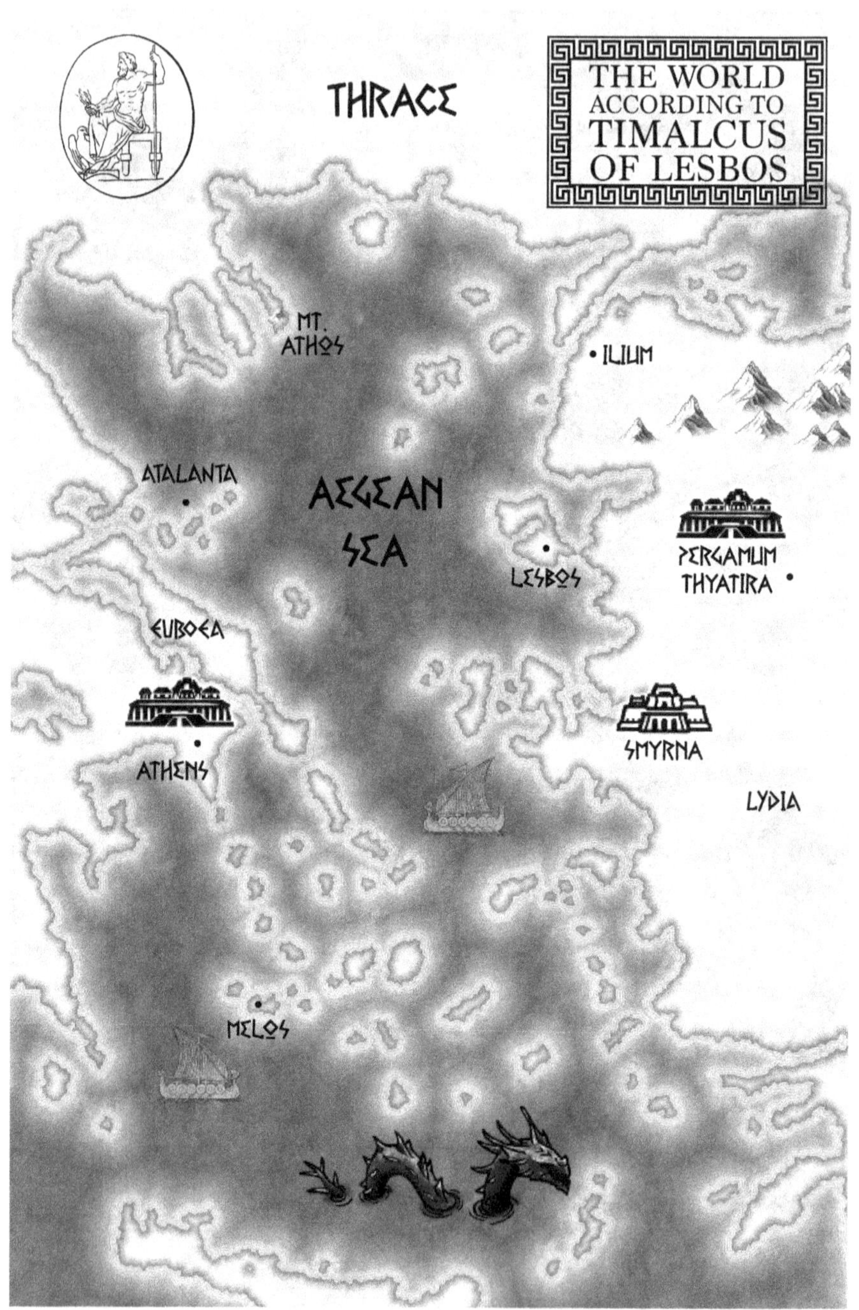
THRACE
THE WORLD
ACCORDING TO
TIMALCUS
OF LESBOS
MT.
ATHOS
ILIUM
ATALANTA
AEGEAN
SEA
LESBOS
PERGAMUM
THYATIRA
EUBOEA
SMYRNA
ATHENS
LYDIA
MELOS

In a different but no less turbulent state of mind, I returned to the harbor, where the Erinyes, fateful Daughters of Night, were already busy with their customary, ineluctable synchronization of punishment.

As Melisanthe's ship caught the tide, an Athenian trireme, bronze battering prow gleaming in the sun and its triple banks of oars canted skyward, glided into port. Its size and power could have only one meaning: Lesbos was called to arms for resumption of the war against Sparta.

When the people of Mytilene had gathered in the agora, the Athenian envoy addressed us. He spoke of new provocations by the Spartans. He reminded us of the unfortunate execution of those thousand Lesbian men who'd rebelled against Athens twelve years ago. But today, he said, Athens knew us as staunch and willing partners in their coalition, eager to join them in a just war. The two ships required of Lesbos must sail at dawn, for one state still clung foolishly to the hope that neutrality was yet an option. They and any other reluctant ally would soon learn otherwise, by sword and fire if the gods so ordained. As we speak, he continued, General Alcibiades assembles our fleet to sail against the misguided rebels of Melos.

At daybreak I'd been the happiest of lovers; at noon the most wretched. My only course of action was obvious - I must somehow rescue Melisanthe. That my father would understand and assist me was implausible, and in any case, he would not oppose my mother. I walked home slowly, practicing an argument which surely, which must, persuade her.

I found her in the garden, directing my sisters in the braiding of garlands.

Mother, I said, the ships ...

Yes, I've already heard. It's war again. But we'll be safe enough here.

But I've decided, I said. I must go. I'm old enough, now - I want to serve, to fight for my country!

She burst out laughing, my sisters, too. You – a solider?

I felt my face burning. I'm a grown man! I shouted. You can't stop me! Unhelpfully for my manly charade, I began to sob, shamefully blubbering like a child.

Mother stared at me. Melos, that's where they're headed. That's it, isn't it? Where your little sweetiepie is going, the chubby tomboy with no common sense? You little fool. Go and lie down, you'll feel better.

I had never had a particularly warm relationship with my mother, but at that moment I could have killed her.

Blind with tears and fury and helplessness, I stomped away. She was right, though, in a way - I'd been a fool to count on her sympathy. But I was still boy enough then to need some approval, some validation, and it came to me suddenly where I might find it.

Mother was a patron of the Orphic Mysteries and I had been once with her to the oracle at Antissa, though I wasn't allowed inside. Divine Orpheus had followed his true love to Hades - surely he would understand my plight. Taking what funds I had, I hitched the pony cart and set out for the north-west coast.

The highway led through fields of barley and orchards of apple and pomegranate, past dark groves where country folk hung bits of horn and shell to Pan among the ivy-berries. At Antissa the road widened to accommodate stalls selling re-freshments for tourists, souvenirs and votive offerings which those too poor to visit the oracle itself might pray over and lay among the rocks near the temple.

Past the town I came to the sacred grove of alder trees where stands the shrine of Orpheus's Head. Orpheus, patron of song and rhyme, it is said, was torn limb from limb by the stag-priestesses of Thrace. His head was still singing when they flung it in the Hebrus, from whence the river and the seatides bore it to the coast of Lesbos. Here, where it made landfall, this ancient temple was carved.

No other supplicants were waiting; only a few drowsy bees stirred the clearing. While I watered my pony, an attendant went to fetch the priest, who presently emerged.

I have a question, I said. An urgent one, I must consult the sibyl right away.

He cast a doubtful look at me, the anxious, dusty youth before him. My mother is Perseana, I told him - she comes here quite often. From my purse I withdrew my largest coin, a silver Mytilenian demi-stater bearing Apollo's bust and, appropriately, the lyre of Orpheus. I hadn't time to obtain a proper sacrifice, I said. May I donate this to the temple instead?

Fine, said the priest. I know your mother well, a good client. Come this way, young man. Your first visit on your own, I take it? There is much to see...

At the doorway we washed our hands in a stone basin and entered the antechamber. I must sign the guest register, and I fidgeted nervously while the attendant fetched ink and stylus. On the scroll I saw my mother's name, along with others from the town.

Look at this, the priest said proudly. Running his thumb down the rows of faded signatures. He pointed out the name of Sappho, in Aeolic script, and beside it what he insisted was that of Homer, himself. My first impulse was to argue that to visit here contemporaneously with Sappho, Homer would have been three hundred years old, but I bit my tongue and pretended to be awed.

And here, he went on, fondling the most ancient scroll, you will scarcely believe this, but the very first signature is by Herakles! They were great friends, you know, Orpheus and Herakles. Just imagine!

At length we started down a narrow passage lined with lamplit niches, each handsomely painted with scenes from the life of Orpheus: him quelling the sirens from Argo's deck, his marriage, Eurydice with the viper that slew her, Orpheus in Hades, and so forth. The priest was visibly disappointed when I said I hadn't time just now to admire them.

Very well, then. You may wait in the gift shop while I summon the sibyl. Try the cheese - it's delicious.

The room he indicated was lined with shelves and tables of various goods for sale: busts of Orpheus and of Eurydice, pottery bearing the legend "Souvenir of Antissa," bread and cheese, miniature lyres and so on. Two women were embroidering shirts reading "My Parents Brought Me This Tunic From The Oracle." I was just paying for a bit of cheese and bread for the journey home when the priest returned.

Now in full sacerdotal regalia, he beckoned me with grave formality, took my arm and led me into the temple.

The passage opened into the stony chamber of the antron, where smoldering torches cast a deliberately theatrical chiaroscuro. A rock-cut ledge, from the crevices of which issued a nauseous, saffron vapor, made a podium across the rear wall. The air stank of smoke and naphtha and sulfur.

My host showed me where to stand, then dragged a three-legged stool onto the ledge, placing it over the stream of rising gas. He led the sibyl out and helped her seat herself on the tripod.

In the flickering light she seemed a pale and wraithy creature; beneath her veils I could see the limbs of a girl, but her face was a wizened cronemask. The priest held a dish of laurel leaves and other herbs to her and she began to chew them, staring vacantly ahead and occasionally yawning. There emerged from her an audible fart, to which the cave lent an amusing echo, which caused her to snicker briefly.

Ask your question now, boy, said the priest.

How shall I find and rescue my love, Melisanthe?

The sibyl gave a derisive snort. Always the same question, she muttered. Whining lovers. Feh! The boredom is excruciating. Why never a champion, a hero? Bring me the cloak, then.

The priest fetched a robe and draped it over her. I could hear her deeply inhaling the vapor that rose to fill her makeshift tent. Then silence.

A minute passed, then two. From the folds of the cloak came the unmistakable sound of snoring.

With a sigh, the priest rose from his seat, climbed laboriously onto the podium and laid a sharp blow across her back with a green myrtle switch. Instantly she sat upright, flinging off the cloak. Her eyes rolled over blind and white and ribbons of snot coursed from her nostrils.

Behold! cried the priest in triumph. Orpheus comes!

The sibyl began to moan and shudder, then, in a husky voice, to speak:

The tongues of the dead smoke the wind of Icarus;
Drunk on the wine of flight, ascent is your labyrinth.
Thieves commerce in stolen words and finger meaning
Into a text of libelous letters which can't be inked.
Pestilence is the feast time of lice -
Fuel your want with vengeance, and so condemn your children to war ....

With a final shiver she slumped on her stool, wreathed in spiralling fumes. The priest led her away; I could hear her teeth chattering. When he returned to accompany me out, he was ebullient.

You're a lucky lad, he said. She's in fine form today. You don't get a show like that just anywhere, I can tell you that!

It was already dark. I drove the pony home at a reckless pace, puzzling furiously over the words of Orpheus and gnawing at the bread and cheese, which was, in fact, so delicious I regretted not taking some home to Father. By the time I reached Mytilene only the hexameter's last line made any sense to me: the child condemned to war was me.

From my room I took a fresh tunic and cloak and put them in my sack with a cap and spare sandals. As usual, my father was working late in his library.

Aganus, he said. I was looking for you. How goes the mapping?

Very well, Father. I am just coming to work on it.

I took my map from its place and added my mapping tools, inks and brushes to my knapsack. For a moment I stood in the doorway, looking back at him, a scrim of hot tears pestering my eyes. We bade each other good night and I crept away from my father's roof.

My name, of course, is Timalcus. Who Aganus might be is a mystery - there is no one so called in our family. Perhaps my father had once meant to give a son that name and had simply forgotten to do so.

The Lesbian galleys were bright with lamps and torches in the harbor, crowded with men loading and storing amphorae, grainsacks, coils of rope, racks of spears and armor. Another gang smeared the hull with arsenic paste and sulfur oil. I boarded the fifty-oared pentaconter and approached the first officer I saw, volunteering for the campaign.

Get off my deck, pipsqueak, he said crossly.

But I'm young and brave and strong, I said, holding up a thin arm to flex a scarcely visible bulge of muscle.

We're fully crewed. Go home, boy.

And I'm a first class citharode, for my age. I can sing Homer's rhymes, battle songs for soldiers. And I know all the winesongs of Terpander and much of Alkaeus, too.

Perhaps it was some residual blessing of Orpheus, accruing from my visit to the oracle, I thought later, or maybe Cypris

Aphrodite pitied my lovesick heart, but just as this brute was about to toss me into the harbor, the captain walked by. Fate, fortune, who can explain these things?

Stitcher of songs, eh? Turn him loose, said the captain. And the lyre? Can you pipe? Certainly, I lied. A citharode's apprentice, just specify rhythm and tempo.

What will your father say of this?

A great patriot, sir. He'll be shamed if I don't serve. And here I fabricated an implausible military career for both my father and grandfather. And I'm educated, too, I went on. I can read maps, logs, orders....

Here, read this, he said, handing me a roster of the Athenian chain of command. When I'd recited it, I pulled from my cloak the Herodotian map and unrolled it.

You made this?

Yes, I said. And I can read, write and translate every form of Greek and Persian, of Aegyptus, Latin, Old Cretan, Lydian...

Enough! he laughed. Stow your sack and help with those jars. We sail at first tide.

On the Asian coast the first penumbra of violet daybreak crept above the mountains. A sleepy crowd gathered on the docks to watch the hoplites with their clanking shields and helmets board the ships. The coxes cried and banged their drums, boneflutes sang, our oars dipped and foamed the water and the war-galleys of Lesbos lurched from the harbor and slid, Melos bound, onto the winedark sea.

> Think, Lady Moon, how my love came to be.
> Turn, Magic Wheel, and drive my lover home.

Chapter Two

Little Spies

OF THE HORROR ON MELOS I can speak little.

Our swift galleys should have overtaken Melisanthe's vessel no later than the straits of Andros, but the Daughters of Night, or Cronus himself, deprived us of wind and my Lesbian comrades showed no enthusiasm for bending their oars harder to rush more quickly into battle. We were nearly the last ally to reach Melos and the final assault had begun the previous day. The Melians, certain their claim to neutrality was righteous, had trusted the gods to deliver them, but the gods slept that day, or were drunk, or were away pleasuring their loins with some pretty mortal.

As our hoplites were ferried ashore I slipped over the side and swam through a harbor already clotted with corpses. Inside the city walls lay heaps of dead men running blood and shit; their juices stood in pools, thickening and black between the burning houses. Lines of tethered women and girls were led captive through the town, and as I searched their faces I was attacked from behind and clubbed unconscious to earth.

What soldier saved my life I never learned. I awoke on an Argive pinnace as it sailed into Piraeus, and when I was able to walk, went in search of my ship. To my horror, I learned they had already sailed for home, taking with them my money, my clothing ... and my map.

Penniless and stranded, I joined the throng of sailors and archers and hoplites in the long trudge up the walled causeway of Pericles to the city of Athens. From their talk I learned the story of our great victory. Every male on Melos had been put to the sword, and the women and girls taken away as slaves.

I asked an Athenian lieutenant about them.

Domestic slaves, most of them - the old, fat, ugly ones, he said. They'll be sold at market. Some will be whores for the army in the coming campaign.

What about the pretty ones?

Concubines for the generals and politicians. They're not for the likes of us. The beauties and the nobles will be parceled out to the war captains and so-called generals. It has been ever thus since Achilles captured Briseis and then Agamemnon took her from Achilles. Proving that it's best not to get too attached to whores.

And the most beautiful young girls, what of them?

He laughed. Nosey kid, aren't you? Alcibiades, so I've heard, has taken a dozen of the ripest for his own use. Spoils to the victor, as Gillaumus Marcius says.

Where might I find Alcibiades? I'd like to tell them back home that I met the famous general in person.

Oh, he'll be around. All of Athens wants to see him now. For one reason or another.

Guarding the Gate of Pericles were the grim Scythian police who kept order in the city so that no Athenian need ever lay violent hands on a fellow citizen. In the plays of Aristophanes the Scyths were comical barbarians; in real life, they were hard and dangerous. They scrutinized the incoming crowd, questioning some, searching a few, watching for Spartan assassins,

Persian spies and other enemies of the state. At length I was allowed to pass.

Sardis, I had thought, was a great city. Ten times larger and twenty more splendid and bustling was Athens. Often lost, I made my way through the streets. In some quarters my fellow soldiers and I were greeted as heroes and offered food and drink.

From Lesbos, eh? Is it true what they say about your women? Some claim Corinthian pussy is the best, but I've heard those Lesbian girls will fuck a man dry and beg for more. Come, lad, have some wine!

But it was a divided city. In other streets soldiers were given hostile stares, and I heard speeches denouncing Alcibiades and the assembly which had empowered him. Half of Athens was jubilant; over the other half hung a palpable cloud of shame.

At the Theater of Dionysus, I stopped to admire the gleaming new Parthenon high above, austere in form but gaudy and cheerful in its lacquered coats of crimson and green and sky-blue paint. I would take Melisanthe to see it after I had found her and rescued her, holding her precious hand and keeping her close by my side as we strolled. She would be grateful, adoring.

By this time I had it firmly fixed in my mind that since Melisanthe had undoubtedly been among the most beautiful captives taken on Melos, it must certainly be Alcibiades himself into whose possession she had fallen. In those neighborhoods where it seemed safe to do so, I inquired about him.

A most unpredictable fellow, said a flower seller. Comes and goes as he pleases, he and his entourage, appears suddenly before the assembly, gives a speech, then whisks off to the theater or the races. Or his whores or intrigues or his parties. But he will certainly visit his old friend and mentor, Sokrates. Find Sokrates and you'll soon enough get a look at the general.

He gave me directions to the agora and advised me to search among the stoa for an ugly old man holding colloquy with a circle of young admirers. He's a gruesome old gnome, the wisest man in Athens some say, the greatest fool according to others, he went on. Quite possibly, both at once.

I knew of this Sokrates. My father and I had read his *Ethikos*, and I also knew his bawdy comic play on marriage. He proved easy to find, and as I'd been warned, was not a pretty sight. I was taught not to judge men by appearance, but Sokrates was short, bandy-legged, with Nubian lips, a squashed turnip nose and bulging frog-like eyes. He had a striking, hypnotic quality: it was as hard to turn away as it was to look at him. When I joined the group around him he was addressing an unhappy looking young man.

Yes or no, said Sokrates. Would you allow a single mindless beast to make our laws?

Of course not.

And yet the demos, the vast, nattering, unwashed, unlettered public, are, as you've agreed, illogical and easily swayed. How then is a herd of ignorant apes better qualified than a single one to govern?

But, said the boy stubbornly, the very definition of democracy, of citizenship, is that the opinion of every qualified citizen must be considered. The greater good is achieved only ....

The greater good, Sokrates explained, is that you shut up.

The others murmured approval as the young troublemaker slunk away.

Children today are such tyrants, Sokrates sighed. They contradict their teachers and tyrannize their parents. In my day, children knew their places. I shudder to think of the future.

One of the students looked past me into the crowd. Oh no, he said, here comes Big Head!

Or Fathead, you might call him, said Sokrates to much laughter.

Why do you call him that? I asked, turning to see a boy approaching, a stocky, redfaced lad with no discernible neck and what was indeed a strikingly large forehead.

Sokrates regarded me for a moment, feigning great seriousness.

Well, he said, just look at the size of that noggin. Why, his brain must be enormous!

His retinue laughed even harder as the boy joined our circle and stood with an uncertain smile.

Androcles, greetings, Sokrates said pleasantly. It's time, I've just decided, that if you are to join our akademia one day, you must have a new name, a proper scholar's name. Henceforth you will be known among us as Plato.

Androcles frowned. I don't get it, he said.

"Broad of brow" is an apt translation, said Sokrates.

Just then a stout woman sprang from the passing crowd, seizing him by the ear.

Here you are, lazy rascal! she cried. You're coming with me, to look for work, as promised!

We all stepped clear of the struggle.

She twisted his ear so viciously that he bent nearly double and dropped the wine he'd been sipping. Help, boys! he cried, Old Horse Lips has got hold of me again!

Twisting harder, she pulled him into the street.

Ow! Ow! he yelped. I'll be back later, he called over his shoulder, if the old ball and chain permits ....

The rest of his words were drowned out by the market noise as she dragged him away.

Didn't put up much of a fight this time, observed one of the students. Remember the time she ripped his cloak and mantle clear off him? He still wouldn't budge.

Well, said another, he was in the middle of a lecture on Epistemo-logical Heuristics that day. He was really on a roll.

As the group dispersed I was left alone with Plato, formerly Androcles. I asked him who the woman was.

That's Xanthippe, his wife. I'm supposed to keep an eye out for her. I'm probably in the doghouse for missing her today.

Why did he call her ...

Horse Lips? Her name means "Mighty Horse." Sometimes he calls her Old Nag or Horse Hips. He likes puns.

Yes, so I gather.

You're new here, aren't you? he asked me.

I told him briefly how I'd come to Athens, and that I urgently needed to find Alcibiades.

That won't be easy, he said. But I know his house, one of them anyway. I'll take you there.

He led me from the agora past the Temple of The Twelve Gods, through the ceramics quarter and the Sacred Gate, heading, he explained, for the district of finer homes.

What shall I call you? Androcles or Plato?

He frowned, concentrating intensely for a few moments. Plato, I guess. Yes, Plato. That means "broad of brow," you know.

I didn't disagree.

As we walked, he told me about himself. He was eleven years old and a champion wrestler, a sport for which his stout, compact body was ideal. In a few years, though, he would abandon the path to Olympic glory and become a full-time pupil of Sokrates. The life of a philosopher was his dream. In the meantime he served the teacher as he could.

What do you do for him?

Bring him wine, Plato said. He guzzles all day long but never gets drunk. Sometimes I help the other boys discourage ignorant people from voting. Fetch him bread - he won't accept money, you know. Here we are, this is Alcibiades's house.

We stood before a sprawling villa surrounded by gardens and statuary, with extensive stables nearby for the general's famous horses and chariots. On the portico stood two uni-formed guards.

By the way, said Plato, you never said what you want with Alcibiades.

When I explained, he frowned. I don't get it, he said. Then he shrugged and pulled me towards the house. Come on, you're going to need my help.

I trembled as I stood before the guards.

I am Timalcus, I said, soldier of Lesbos. There has been a terrible mistake. The most beautiful of the general's new slaves taken on Melos is not a native Melian. She's an inno-cent Lesbian girl, and I have full authority from the archons of Mytilene to return her to her family.

They roughed us up only a little as they threw us into the street; it was less painful than their laughter. After we had recovered a bit, Plato bade me farewell and rose to go - it was nearly dusk. Then he turned back.

Where will you sleep?

In the agora, I suppose. I can find my way back there, I think.

You're coming home with me, he said, pulling me to my feet.

And that is how I came to Plato's house and met his par-ents, and how, when they learned of my skills as linguist and scholar, they hired me, for a room in the servants' quarters, meals and two obols a week, as tutor to their son.

Plato and I got on well together. He tackled our studies with the tenacity of a wrestler, and though he had strong opinions of his own, listened to me for the most part with respect, feel-ing for me, I think, the sort of affectionate responsibility a boy feels for a stray dog he's rescued.

He was keen on politics, of which I knew little; loved all things historical and was fascinated with the physical nature of the cosmos. That Earth was very likely a sort of globe we agreed, that it was a flat disc atop a cylinder unlikely and that it moves around the sun preposterous. Pythagoras's notion of Opposite Earth, replete with boiling seas and monstrosities, intrigued us both, though neither of us could figure out why those people walking about upside down didn't just fall off.

But he detested Homer. Portraying the gods and goddesses as immoral and malicious was blasphemous, he said. Gods, he insisted, must be perfect, ideals to which we can aspire, not naughty, lascivious children. And Achilles, he said, don't get me started on Achilles! What a crybaby! Blubbering and pouting over some girl. What a lousy role model for Greek men!

Here I knew something most Greeks would have found deeply heretical, but I decided to share it with Plato.

Homer makes him a Greek, of course, but Achilles is not a Greek name. Its etymological roots lie in the East, in Asia Minor, most likely in Phrygia, according to my research, I told him.

You're making that up, he exclaimed. Well, on second thought, maybe that explains it - he was some effete eastern dude, probably a Persian dandy.

And so went our days.

In the evenings, though, after I had dined with the other servants and Plato with his family, he and I would slip from the house and go in search of Alcibiades.

We went first to the house from which we'd been driven by the guards, studying each window from the darkness of the gardens. We identified the harim, confirming, as was widely rumored, that Alcibiades had exotic oriental tastes and habits. Many lovely young men and girls appeared therein, but none so beautiful as Melisanthe.

But Alcibiades, we learned, had a second home of his own, another for his wife and kept still others for his mistresses as well. We watched each in turn, hoping for clues. One night as we kept vigil in a bower of honeysuckle, Plato asked me about Melisanthe. I tried to describe her beauty and my love for her and the terrible desperation I felt.

I don't get it, he said. Anyway, Sokrates says the state should select mates for us, to improve the species.

You haven't fallen in love yet, I said. Perhaps when you're as old as I am - fourteen - you'll understand. But imagine it this way: we are born as two conjoined beings, one male, one female, with two heads, four arms, and so on. But we were chopped in half at birth.

Ugh, that's disgusting. Who did the chopping?

I don't know - the gods maybe.

Why would they do that?

The gods do cruel and pointless things all the time, Plato. But that's not the point.

No they don't. Despite Homer and the other godmockers, any deity must be pure and benign.

Okay, maybe, I said. But the point is that this other being is part of us, our missing other half. And to be truly happy we must be reunited. So we must search for her. Or him. It's our nature, our destiny, our human imperative.

Is that what love is like?

"Love, that loosener of limbs, bittersweet and inescapable crawling thing," I said. That was Sappho.

Wow, Plato said. I don't get the point of most poetry, but that was pretty good.

He went silent for a time. Okay, he said at last, I get it - it's a romantic thing.

From time to time we saw Alcibiades himself. He often hosted loud, drunken parties, and he and his retinue would sometimes erupt merrily into the streets in the dark morning hours and wander about Athens, banging on gates, waking friends and demanding wine, playing practical jokes and creating mischief. He was easy to pick from the group, a strikingly handsome man wearing a bizarre and distinctive costume: an oversized woman's robe of royal purple trailing a filthy, bedraggled hem over which, with much cursing and laughing, he occasionally stumbled and fell. Two boys ran beside him with jugs of wine to refill the sloshing goblet with which he anointed their path.

We learned, too, to pick out his voice - he spoke with a pronounced lisp widely imitated by his aristocratic young admirers, though not in his presence. As he strolled he kept up a patter of witty gossip and repartee. His cleverness could not be denied, but Plato and I felt that his sense of humor tended towards the cruel and sarcastic, and therefore lacked the comity and refinement of a true gentleman.

Much of the general's background was well known. Of noble family, he was a nephew to the great Pericles. He'd been one of Sokrates's most brilliant students; the two had served together in the war, even sharing a camp blanket on occasion, whereof Alcibiades had been forced to admit that Sokrates was the only person he'd ever tried and failed to seduce. His horses and chariots were legendary in Olympic history, and on their fame, family connections and undisputed skill as orator, he had built his career as statesmen and soldier.

This had made him enormously wealthy. Many rich Athenians boasted fifty slaves; Alcibiades was thought to have a hundred, with fifty concubines besides. He kept a dozen mistresses, a Persian major domo for each house and Libyan eunuchs to tend his harim. His business pursuits generated a voluminous stream of correspondence over which he exercised much secrecy. When attending to these papers, he kept beside him an Aegyptus dwarf to whom he fed the letters after reading them, so that no one might discover their contents. The product of the dwarf's bowels, he often remarked, compared favorably with the literary output of Euripides, whose liberal opinions he loathed.

Many were the handsome young men and women we watched him share a couch with. He had no scruple but to fornicate where and when the mood took him and in whatever company he found himself. But the face I sought among his conquests did not appear. One night, in order to get a definitive look at one girl, Plato insisted on climbing a fig tree outside his window. The limb gave way and he fell booming into a koi pond - we were nearly caught. I returned him to his house soaked and laughing, exhilarated by his adventure. He was, withal, a good sport if a bit clumsy.

Due to our studies, Plato and I had few opportunities to stalk Alcibiades at his daytime appearances. He made speeches to the assembly and elsewhere, and to mitigate the citizens' disapproval of his scandalous behavior, often gave lavish public entertainments with much free food and wine. At one such gathering we tried to approach him directly, but were prevented from doing so by his bodyguards and the ever present circle of followers around him.

Plato still attended most of Sokrates's daily lectures while I stayed home to read. One such day he returned with stunning news.

You missed him, Plato said. Alcibiades was there, too bad. It was really funny, though. Sokrates nailed him good!

Cursing my luck, I asked what had happened.

Alcibiades, it seemed, had been bragging about his wealth, especially all the farms and villas and orchards he owns. So Sokrates took out this map ...

Map?

A map of the world, something like Herodotus. And he challenged Alcibiades to show us all his properties. On that scale, of course, they were too tiny to see, mere pinpricks. He left in a huff, and we all laughed.

What sort of map? I said. Describe it.

Oh, about this big. Vellum, or calfskin parchment, very fine. It showed Greece, Sparta, the Aegean down to Aegypt and Libya and pretty far east.

The meridional projection was centered about where? Lesbos, perhaps?

Maybe, Plato said. That seems about right.

Where is Sokrates? I demanded. Gone home? Take me there straight away.

In the dooryard of Sokrates's home two small children sat in the dirt, toying with a cat who clearly wished he was elsewhere. Plato pulled the bell.

When Sokrates let us in, I spotted my map immediately, lying on a table. I stepped past him and began to unroll it.

Where did you get this?

Oh, that's mine, Sokrates said. I made that.

No, you didn't. Here is my sign, my name on it - Timalcus of Lesbos.

He studied me for a moment. Well, well, you're right - this isn't my map, mine is much better. It's around here some-where. This map I bought fair and square from a sailor just returned from Melos.

Xanthippe appeared in a doorway. Give the boy his map, she said.

How much? I opened my purse.

Value is a fascinating concept, Sokrates said. Possession, bill of sale, provenance, all that. I might cover this complicated question in a lecture next week if you like.

Three obols were all I had. I laid them on the table and stood glaring angrily at him.

Finders keepers, he said.

Xanthippe stepped farther into the room. I said, give the boy his map, you damned old fool!

Ah, the sound of wifely thunder, Sokrates said. We'd best step outside, boys, there's going to be a rumpus.

He hustled us out into the courtyard. Really, boys, this is a matter better discussed at the stoa. Coming to my home like this makes me a bit cross ....

Xanthippe stepped from the doorway bearing a pisspot, which she emptied on her husband's head, then darted back inside.

He stood there dripping for a moment. Well, he said, after thunder, then comes the rain. Say, that's pretty good! I should write that down.

His wife reappeared and thrust my map at me. Here, take it and go, she said, glancing at Sokrates. He'll be all right...

I was overcome with joy at regaining my beloved map, but Plato was silent on the way home. He never spoke of the incident, though in the coming days I noticed he went less often to hear the teachings of Sokrates.

Determined never to lose possession of my map again, I constructed a quiver of oxhide for it, lined with oilskin, glued at one end with a thonged cap above, and secured it with a stout shoulder strap.

Plato was much taken with the map. I showed him the intricate play of rhumb line and meridian, and how to use the Aegyptus circle and compass, encouraging him to try his own hand at the craft. We spent many hours scanning the travels of Herodotus and revising a bit where he'd gone astray. Plato's father had a decent library from which we were able to cull a few more geographical tidbits.

From time to time his father received texts from his old friend, Thucydides, sent to Athens for safekeeping. Having failed badly as a general, Thucydides had been exiled, and was currently writing a history of the war, which Plato and I were allowed to read.

In the summer of the war's sixth year, he had written, a series of very large earthquakes occurred, causing great damage and impeding the Athenian campaign. Off the coast of

Euboea, the sea had retreated, then flung itself upon the land, and a tidal wave had swallowed the entire island of Atalanta, along with the ships there stationed. For some reason, Plato became obsessed with this story. Just imagine! he would say. A whole island, a city-state, every person, every house, an entire population, swept away in an instant!

I tried to tell him that such things have always happened, that the anger of Poseidon has always been with us, but he kept marvelling over it and could not get it out of his head for a long time. I just hope he forgets about it, and doesn't do something foolish with it.

Meanwhile, Alcibiades continued to lobby Athens with various plans to defeat Sparta. He proposed a massive southern wall for which the Spartans would somehow pay. No one believed this scheme. His idea to cripple Sparta by conquering Sicily, their primary source of grain, however, met with more success. Through his stirring speeches, public largesse and, it was rumored, a few cunningly placed bribes, he secured the assembly's approval, and the fleet prepared for war. Then things went horribly wrong for Alcibiades. Sole command of the expedition was denied him; a hated rival would share his rank. Even in public, he did not bother to conceal his fury.

For this flawed victory he nevertheless held a celebration, a banquet at which Plato and I kept our customary surveillance. Past midnight the revelers burst forth, carrying not only their supply of drink, but an assortment of masons' tools. We followed as the general and his cronies, with conspiratorial whispers and snickering, reeled down the street. Before the house of Euripides, whose latest play had rebuked the Athenians for the shame of Melos and presented a scathing satire of Alcibiades, they halted. Alcibiades entered the courtyard and we heard the sharp crack of hammer on stone; when he returned moments later whatever he joked to his friends provoked laughter. After they had moved on, we crept inside. He had ignored the altar of Athene - not even Alcibiades dared profane that goddess in her own city - and instead chosen a marble Hermes, whose miniature penis he had clumsily amputated.

For two hours they roamed the streets, unmanning Hermes wherever they found him. Plato and I had seen enough. You must inform the archons at first light, I told him as we neared his home.

Why me? I don't get it.

I'm a foreigner. Your family is well respected - they'll believe you.

But why? Who cares anymore about Alcibiades and his silly pranks?

Think, Plato. After Athene, who is more beloved of Athens than sweet, gentle Hermes? Perhaps this time they'll arrest Alcibiades and his cohorts. Then we'd have a better chance of gaining entry to his homes and finding Melisanthe. Anyway, they've blasphemed. It's your duty to report them.

I'll do it, Plato said. Not for love, for respect of the gods.

By that afternoon, when everyone knew of the collection of phalluses left in a mocking heap on the steps of the Erechtheum, the public's titillation with the excesses of Alcibiades had turned to outrage. The archons were compelled to act, but by the time they came to arrest him it was too late; he'd sailed for Syracuse, his flagship leading a steady stream of long black ships from the harbor of Piraeus.

Only servants, slaves and concubines remained at the homes of Alcibiades and his mistresses. Where there was resistance, Plato plowed them aside like a young bullock. But not one of the dozens we spoke to had heard the name Melisanthe or remembered the girl with emerald eyes.

But their master, they said, had taken with him his seven favorites.

What will you do now? Plato asked.

I must follow, my friend. What else can I do?

Plato's father, vouching for the same talents that had earned my passage from Lesbos and his patronage as Plato's pedagogue, secured a place for me on the last ship to leave Athens, a fifty-oared galley from Mykonos. It bore a company of Athenian policemen who had patriotically volunteered - Scythian archers, descendants of mighty Herakles it's said, the world's finest bowmen.

Plato was a tough kid, but there were tears in his eyes as we said our farewells. He was a good friend to me and I wished him success, though as I told him then, he should probably stick to wrestling.

The coxcall boomed, our oars churned foam in the harbor and we pulled out against the winedark tide into the Saronic Sea. As I unrolled my map to show the captain, I mused on this new fate, this second voyage, to Sicily, beyond which my chart was inked more in dreams and myth than certainty.

Off the coast of Troezen, Nev, sergeant-at-arms of the Scythians, approached with two of his men. They seized the captain, slit his throat and threw him into the sea. Two of the Mykonian crew who resisted met the same fate. We shipped oars, paid out our sheets and the helmsman swung our black prow to port. A fresh wind drove us north against the drumming salt spray as the last ships of the Athenian flotilla rapidly disappeared astern, carrying Melisanthe and her foul abductor away to the unknown ends of earth. Helplessly I felt my map unscrolling itself beneath me, wickedly bearing me away towards destinations not of my own choosing.

Think, Lady Moon, how my love came to be.
Turn, Magic Wheel, and drive my lover home.

Chapter Three

The Scyths

NEV, THE DE-FACTO CAPTAIN, took my map but soon found he needed my help in deciphering it. Each time he consulted me I begged him to put me ashore, but after he cuffed me to the deck a few times I gave up pleading and began to think of escape. We sailed up the coasts of Euboea and Magnesia, crossed the Myrtoan Sea and rounded Mount Athos on the Macedonian headlands, where the gods took away our wind. Looping our oars to the tholepins, we stripped naked in the heat and in three days time rowed the length of Thrace. Off the plains of windy Troy we moored to rest, and Nev saw me eyeing the shore.

I have other plans for you, boy, he said, chaining me to the thwart for the long pull up the Hellespont's current. So shackled I remained through the Sea of Propontis, past Byzantium and beyond the Clashing Rocks, following Jason and Herakles and neglectful Orpheus into the black Euxine, and thence along its southern coast towards the rising sun. Here my geography was less reliable, and Nev slapped me about for each discrepancy. Had I not already demonstrated other skills, he would surely have thrown my carcass to the fishes.

Thus, on we sailed, bound for one far corner of the known world while Melisanthe, so I believed, languished at the other.

On a bright afternoon in spring we made port at the Milesian colony of Trapezus. The harbor was crowded with Greek ships bringing wine and Parian marble and copper from Cyprus to trade for wheat and amber, for jade and spices from the east and for the famous gold of Colchis. Here, I was sure, lay my transport back to civilization, but when Nev sold the ship and its crew he kept me at his side, leashed like a wayward pup. Outside the city walls more Scythians, tattooed, fierce and long of hair, waited for us with horses, and the next morning we left the coast, heading, I was told, towards the mountains of Armenia, or as some call it, Urartu.

Inland from Trapezus lies the Valley of Khorsat, where the way begins to rise steeply in a narrow, twisting trail above rocky gorges. Mist from the booming sea rose beside us, turning into thick clouds before our eyes; snow and ice lay all about us. We gained the pass - it is called Zagana - from which one might glimpse a last view of the coast if the clouds ever broke. The icy wind which thrust us up then diminished, and we came down among gray foothills. The peak just to our east was Mount Theches, a place holy to the Macronians who live in mud huts below it, and who are famous for cutting the throats of travellers and taking their heads for sport and display. The mountain itself is a place of pilgrimage, with small shrines dotting its slopes.

Here, in a hillside meadow, we joined a band of Nev's Scythian kinsmen. Their greeting left no doubt that he was a man of some stature among them.

I knew, or thought I knew, something of the Scyths from Herodotus; the Royal Scyths, the settled northern farmers and various nomadic tribes, some of whom were traders who ranged as far south as Luristan to acquire their famous bronze blades. But there were other bands, raiders and bandits, and it soon became clear that it was among this much more dangerous clan I had landed.

Our arrival brought the band's number to just over a hundred. A dozen or so women stood aside, in long gowns to which small golden plaques were sown, and much clanking jewelry as well. I thought the rest all men, but discovered women among them, both sexes tattooed on every visible surface: elk and wolf and creatures of fantasy. All wore long riding boots and, at their waists, red sashes from which hung an assortment of knives or hatchets and elaborately carved hand mirrors. From time to time they would pause and gaze solemnly into these glasses, not for vanity, but some sort of religious observance, so I learned. Their tunics were bright and garish Kashmiri silk and every man and woman bore earrings and bells and jewels. All of them stank of sweat and dust and horses, a pungent odor more accented than diminished by the coatings of crushed coriander with which they lavishly powdered themselves.

Cups and goblets, some fashioned from human skulls, were brought out and filled. The Scyths drank unwatered wine and mare's milk fermented in goatskin bags, and were soon very drunk. They began to wrestle and box and, all in play, to bash one another with cudgels.

They seemed as wild and unpredictable as bloodcrazy satyrs, and I sat cowering in their mad, howling, inebriated, brawling midst, too frightened to move. Like Orpheus, I had tried to follow my love into hell - the hell of war, of Sicily, so I had thought. Instead I'd fetched up in the hell of a barbarian wilderness, where I expected momentarily to further imitate Orpheus by being hacked into bloody scraps. That I would then burst into song, as he had, seemed far less likely.

Out of this melee a singular creature staggered. Over his tunic he wore a cape sewn of human scalps, his blond hair hung in long braids and his face was dark with wine and malice. Eyes locked on me, he lurched forward. I tried to run but he was quickly on me, hands closing on my throat.

I'm going to kill you to hell, he said.

Nev appeared beside us, tugging at the man's arms.

No, Droikha, no, he said. This is the boy I told you of. He can read things and knows many tongues. He is useful...

My assailant dropped one hand to his waist, raised his mirror and stared into it with an expression of intense curiosity, the single fist still at my neck proving more than adequate to the task of strangling me. Just as Nev's pleading seemed likely to end the attack, the man turned his wide eyes back to mine, dropped his looking glass and dug both thumbs into my windpipe. I'm going to kill you to wormshit, he said.

As I passed out Nev and another man were whacking away at him with clubs and trying to pry his fingers from my throat.

After I woke up, they all left me alone. This is how I met Droikha the Void.

At dusk the Scyths laid larch saplings over a firepit and covered them with oxhides to make a sweat chamber. They crawled inside, threw bundles of hemp on the flames and bathed in the smoke. Their shamans put on masks of elkskin and headdresses of bone and antler and called their gods into camp. Late into the night they danced and drank and howled and drummed. Despite the racket, and my fear, I fell at last into exhausted sleep.

At dawn the Scythians, seemingly unaffected by their night of revelry, rose and broke camp with practiced efficiency. I went ahead with the riders, southeast, moving light and fast; the wagons would follow. In four days' time we came to the valley of the Araxes River, and in the foothills above it, where abundant grass and a natural spring provided forage and water for our stock, we dug firepits and latrines, sleeping rough until the wagons arrived a few days later. I was assigned one to sleep in but the stink and chatter of the other occupants drove me out. As it remained fair and warm, I slept beneath it on a horse-hair pallet.

Much of the landscape was unknown to me, but the Araxes, already roughly sketched on my map, was a major trade route from Bactria and the Hindu Kush and from Babylon and Persia to the south, past our encampment and on north to Colchis, Trapezus and the other Euxine ports, from whence one might sail farther west to Byzantium and the Aegean. The spot af-forded tactical control of a long stretch of the valley, and the Scyths seemed to know the area well.

Days and nights of waiting followed. No further drunken feasts were held, but at night their citharodes played a two-stringed lyre they called a gusle, and sang long, lugubrious hero-songs which vibrated in a nasal whine within their throats and drove me to the edge of camp where I sat, hands over my ears, too frightened of wolves to risk a quieter spot in the darkness beyond our firelight.

Hunting parties went out each morning, returning with deer and moose and bear, half of which was roasted, the other half salted and smoked for winter. As Nev ordered, I gathered firewood, tended the horses and oxen, braided horsehair for bowstrings and boiled pitch to feather the Scythians' arrows. Making it known I'd be expected to ride with him when the time came, Nev gave me a good pony, and I was permitted to practice handling her until I had some skill at it. He kept my map but occasionally let me add to it the details of our journey from Athens. Droikha I avoided as much as possible; when he saw me, he scowled, but made no further assault, and none of the others offered me any abuse. As long as I did what I was told and made no trouble I went unnoticed among them.

After a week, a scout returned to announce that a caravan approached from the east. The Scyths got themselves up in leather vests, Kashmir turbans or horned skullcaps and assembled their bows and quivers and hatchets. We descended into the valley.

The travellers had halted, gazing up at the lines of Scythian archers who had silently appeared on both flanks of the valley. Droikha, Nev and I and a few others rode along the river bank, where a few men of the caravan came forward to meet us.

Find out what people they are, Droikha ordered.

I was lucky. A failure to understand them would have given him sufficient excuse to kill me on the spot, but they were Bactrians, with whom I communicated easily.

Tell them to bring out their gods, Droikha said.

When I relayed this command, the Bactrians began to wail piteously and beg for mercy. Even jabs of Scythian daggers did not persuade them to comply, so Droikha dismounted, had their leaders seized and began methodically slicing off their ears and noses. This brought them around, and their deities were unladed and set before us. They were finely wrought Zoroastrian gods of Hindu design, of bronze, copper and electrum, inlaid with chalcedony and moonstone, and the finer pieces were goldplate studded with beryl or ch'uti jade. We emptied one of their oxcarts, loaded their gods within and drove it away. At this, some of the Bactrians fell to the ground, flinging dust on themselves and rending their robes in grief.

It was a large, well provisioned convoy. We took half their oxen, most of their horses, two camels and six handsome young girls, and filled another cart with victuals, bales of Kashmir silk, jars of clove and pepper, a chest of medicinal herbs. Though we left them godless, they had sufficient means to proceed, and to my relief, Droikha let them all live.

That night we held a feast. An ox was tied, strangled, slaughtered and spitted over a firepit, wine flowed in jeweled cups and the gods of Bactria were divested of ruby eyes and beards of black jade. Late in the evening I looked up to find Droikha standing over me.

I'm going to kill you until your bones rattle, he said, but walked on without doing so.

I had no answer to such a remark, though I never doubted that it was a threat he fully meant to carry out one day.

The following weeks were much the same. Caravans large and small continued to pass by, oblivious, it seemed, to the danger. From the west came mostly Greeks from whom I learned some news of the war. From the commercial traders we took blue amber and gold, obsidian and ingots of copper and other wares for sale or barter in the east. Travelling with the merchants were tribal groups and pilgrims whose gods were familiar to me, deities whose theft invariably provoked keening and ululation and histrionics from their devotees. Every group bore weapons, but in the face of Scythian numbers and tactic of ambush there was little resistance, and Droikha felt obliged, mostly for show, to kill only a few, though he left an ample crowfeast of severed ears along the Araxes' banks.

The Scythians' collections of skulls and scalps, and of saddles and capes made from their victims' skins, were taken only in battle, from warriors like themselves, not from such helpless, ignoble folk as these. Nor were ordinary merchants and wayfarers deemed suitable for sacrifice to the gods, a custom rare, but not unheard of among the Scyths.

Caravans from the east were colorful and exotic, and their tongues taxed my skill as a linguist, though I learned a bit more from each one. From an Arabian convoy we appropriated several very fine stallions, a brace of superb falcons, three eunuchs and caches of hazel nuts and opium and various other valuable items, along with a stunning silver fire altar and its resident deity. Bolts of Benares silk, highly prized by the Scyths for its bright colors, we took from a group of Kush Hindus, and a train from Samarkand brought us more fabric, delicious dried fruits, well crafted metal stirrups, goblets and the like, indigo, honey and fish glue. They also had cages of tame marmots, specially trained, so they claimed, to dig out gold. Droikha accused me of mistranslating this, but it turned out to be true.

A second Persian group appeared with an entourage so amazing that everyone from the Scythian camp came down to see it. A young satrap, no more than twelve, rode atop one of three elephants. The boy we kept for ransom; the fate of the great beasts was hotly debated. None of us had ever tasted pachyderm flesh, and there was broad support to utilize this rare opportunity. Nev knew they had considerable value, but also that we could never get them over the pass to Trapezus. The animal proved difficult to kill and awkward to roast, and in the end no one was much pleased with the numerous meals it provided.

There was a convoy from faraway Aegyptus, one of the richest Nev said he'd ever taken. A dozen Abyssinian slaves, yoked like cattle but strong and healthy; a jesting dwarf who Nev allowed us to adopt; lapis, powdered rhinoceros horn, cinnabar and gold; chests of frankincense and myrrh and senna leaf worth a thousand talents - all these we added to our plunder.

Better rolls of Kafir wool and some more common items were shared among our group for rugs and saddles and daily use, but the bulk of our booty was stacked away and held in common. When this hoard of goods and captives and livestock reached sufficient size, Nev began sending convoys of it back to the coast to sell and barter, mainly for gold. This they had the goldsmiths of Colchis smelt and cast along with the pur-loined gods, into jewelry and amulets of Scythian motif. The Scyths were mad for gemstones, more so for gold, those most portable forms of wealth for a nomadic people.

The campaign had proved highly successful, but by mid-summer, traffic along our ambush route was getting sparser - some news of us had likely begun to circulate.

One day we rode down the valley to confront a caravan consisting of a single, threadbare tribe, no more than eighty strong. They had a dozen camels and a few donkeys to carry their possessions: tents, a meager supply of food and little else. The obvious leader – long bearded, grim and ancient - stood before us, and I sought common tongue with him. His language was strange to me, perhaps Semitic or Aramaic in form though ancient beyond my education. As we gabbled at each other an old woman edged her way forward from the rest until she stood just behind him. Droikha stirred impatiently. At length I ventured a line from the K'Habiru epic which the old man recognized, and we began a rudimentary conversation.

He was Shem bar-Yusef, the clan patriarch, he told me. His people were descendants of that tribe made captive by Zargon twelve generations ago.

Thirteen, the old woman said. Shem gave her a dirty look.

Four generations did we dwell in Persia, he went on. Four more among the Medes and another four, blessed be the name of Cyrus the Mashaiya, since we were made free again.

Five, said the woman.

Enough chitchat, Droikha said. Tell them.

I told the K'Habiru to bring out their gods.

Well, Shem said, we have but one.

At this, a faint recollection of the K'Habiru epic returned to me, a memory of one remarkable aspect of that remarkable text.

Your one god, I said, how is he called?

I can't tell you that, the old man said. It's a secret.

When, with some trepidation, I relayed this information to my masters, Droikha spat.

Poor, miserable dogs, he said. Only one god, who lacks even a name. He'd better be a good one.

You'd best surrender him, I told Shem. There will be trouble if you refuse.

He is here with us now, said the patriarch, waving a hand in a gesture which seemed to indicate the surrounding valley, hills and sky. Here, now, always.

The old woman poked his back. Go on, she said, ask him.

With a premonition of impending disaster, I told Shem that their god was not making himself immediately manifest to us, and that if he were not tangibly produced at once, my comrades would almost certainly resort to violence.

The old man drew himself up stiffly into a posture of greater dignity, the effect of which was substantially diminished by his wife's prodding. Well, he said, our god is invisible.

The old lady poked him again, sharply.

Woman, he hissed, keep silent!

I translated Shem's explanation to Nev and the others.

Invisible? said Nev. But that's marvelous!

The Void placed a hand on one of his favorite knives.

Just then the woman shouldered her way past her husband and addressed me: Begging your pardon, Captain, which way is Jebu-Ur-Salim?

What is it? What is the witch saying?

Ur-Salim? I said. In Syria? But you were with the Medes - you had only to travel due west to the coast. How did you wind up five thousand stades to the north?

Shem shrugged. We got turned around, he said.

Expecting the worst, I outlined the K'Habiru's history. Nev, however, was delighted.

Lost? For a century? And the old hag has to ask for directions? He repeated the story to the other riders.

I watched Droikha. Slowly he slid the knife back into his sash. His lips parted in what, though ghastly to behold, must have passed with him as a smile. Then he too began to laugh, an inhuman croak that welled up into a roar of hysteria. His eyes rolled over white and he toppled stiffly from his horse, shuddering convulsively and foaming through clenched teeth. At this, the other Scyths howled with unbound hilarity. They sheathed their weapons and unstrung their bows, collected Droikha and, in merry humor, rode back to camp, leaving the K'Habiru alive, unrobbed and unmolested.

I stayed behind to help the K'Habiru if I could, but Shem refused to listen - their god would guide them, he said. For his wife, though, I drew a map in the river sand and showed her the way to Antiochus, now some five or six thousand stades southwest, from whence it would be a short journey down the coast to Jebu-Ur-Salim. Our scout reported that they'd remained two nights where we left them, arguing and praying, then packed up, turned around and headed back the way they'd come.

Our convoys returned from Colchis and the coast with furs from the north and chests full of new bracelets, rings and pectorals of gold and silver inlaid with bloodstone and other gems giving eyes and claws to the Scythian panther and eagle designs. But no payment came for the captives we'd held for ransom. Droikha strangled the two men and sent the Persian boy and a girl we supposed was some sort of princess to serve among our growing retinue of concubines. There were now some thirty of them, free usage of whom was permitted any member of our band. Nev, who indulged himself often in their company, took me aside one day.

You have a beard now, he said, at least the beginnings of one. Take a whore whenever you like.

I thanked him for the privilege, but declined, explaining that my heart was already given.

Ah, yes - the famous women of Lesbos. Their passion for coupling is quite legendary, is it not?

I've heard that said, I told him. But the truth is that Lesbian women are no more avid for fornication than women anywhere else. It's the gossip of old wives.

Is that so? I often heard the men of Athens say they were the worst. But of course all you Greek men, unless you lie, have little use for fucking. Always complaining about your wives' demands and the high cost of the pacifiers you must provide them. Why are Greek men so sexless?

It's more fashion to pretend so, I think, than reality.

Show me, then. Time for you to enter manhood like a Scythian warrior instead of remaining a Greek pansy.

Alas, I said, my vow of love binds me. You would do me a kindness by not tempting me further.

Nev dropped the matter then, but in truth my reasons for avoiding the concubines were less romantic than I pretended. I had noticed that many of them had rheumy, bloodshot eyes and swollen tongues, and that they visited their latrine with increasing frequency. These observations I kept to myself.

The next caravan came from Persia, and one wagon held a mahogany chest hinting at treasure within. On hacking it open, though, the Scyths found only a bundle of papyrus scrolls which they dumped out on the sand. When the trunk's owner scurried to reclaim them, Nev suspected they must have some value, and confiscated them. That night he called me to his wagon to examine their contents.

There were legal documents, plays and histories and inventories, genealogies of both men and horses, treatises on herbs and medicines, maps of Persian lands and of Bactria and the other Kushan kingdoms, illustrated bestiaries and designs for mechanical devices. One of the latter caught Nev's eye.

This one, he said. What sort of foolish gizmo is this?

I studied the drawing, fascinated.

King Uzziah of Judah had these, three hundred years ago, according to the K'Habiru epic. And Herodotus says that when Cambyses invaded Aegyptus...

Yes, yes, but what is it?

A kata-pelte, I said. Literally, shield piercer. Or lithobolos, stone thrower.

Nev slapped me, glaring. For the last time, he said, what is the damned thing?

It's like a sort of battering ram, that flies. I dodged his next blow. It can throw stones, great heavy stones to knock down the walls of a city ...

He had some difficulty comprehending the concept of scale, but eventually I calmed him down and made him understand that the machine itself would be much larger than the sketch. To stay in his good graces, over the next week I built him a working miniature of it with which he was much pleased. He used to carry it about with him, practicing with pebbles, and guarded it jealously from the others.

Having no further use for the scrolls, Nev gave them to me. For weeks I'd had nothing to read; this small library was a priceless blessing from the gods and at every opportunity I pored over them, not least the maps, by which, with ink and brushes I'd crafted myself, I corrected and extended my own.

Then one day Nev, cross and bored, decided that my other duties were neglected. He dragged me to the firepit and mocked my weeping as he tossed the scrolls one by one into the flames. A sudden, murderous rage welled up in me, a seething hatred directed less at Nev himself than at the cruel barbarian ignorance that invested him and his tribe. I suppressed the feeling but its intensity left me shaken, and after that day I no longer cared to make the Scyths a gift of my tears.

Another day of fire and weeping soon followed. What I had noticed among the concubines gradually became apparent to my captors, and one night in the month of Boedromion they held a council to discuss it.

The next morning I was ordered to help dig a shallow pit. The girls and the little Persian boy, clutching their blankets and clothing, were herded into the depression where they knelt, keening and begging their various gods for deliverance. The Scyths gathered around. Methodically they strung their bows and fitted arrows and, in neither haste nor doubt, slew all the concubines to death. When the pit was silent we slathered pitch across the heap of bodies and laid torches to it. All that day and night the flames cracked and a sick, oily smoke drifted over camp. In the dawn a charred tangle of limbs, of hot ash and blackened skulls remained. This we covered over with a thin veil of dirt while the shamans banged their drums and sang a prayer for fresh booty, for the speedy appearance of a new caravan ripe and fat with jewels and women and gold.

In truth, the wayfarers we robbed had begun to seem much the same to me, and I lost count of their numbers and home-lands. But one tribe we met held special interest - they were followers of Pnum, whose vedas I had read.

They came from Gujarat, in the empire of Nanda, in India, the sunburnt ends of earth. Pnum, it turned out, was a squat, reptilian creature with fangs and an unpleasant leer, cast crudely in rough terracotta. Droikha kicked at it in disgust, discovering that it was suspiciously heavy. He chipped the clay shell away to reveal a statue cast in fine silver with eyes of Badakshan lapis set in emerald takhtis, making him a prize worth our efforts. Clearly it was the only item of any value they possessed, but this tribe grieved less at their loss than any I'd seen - their sorrow seemed strangely perfunctory. This lack of emotion saved them further suffering as well. Spared the annoyance of their wailing, Droikha let them pass with ears and limbs largely intact.

That night another feast was held to celebrate that taking of silver Pnum and seven new concubines, whose favors the Scyths were already utilizing. Nev, having already sported one of them, was relaxed, and the wine made him more chatty than usual. I sat down beside him and asked about his co-captain, Droikha.

Why is he called the Void?

The Droikha you see now, the fits of weeping and rage, the habit of swaying, the bouts of narcolepsy, the violence, these are not what he once was, Nev said. Seven years ago he was our clan's most beloved singer. He played the gusle with great feeling and rhymed songs of our heroes which brought tears to our eyes. Then one night a man named Kursa said something which Droikha felt insulted his playing. They fought a duel; Droikha didn't die, though. He got conked on the noggin. But it was his own fault, anyway.

Why?

Kursa's remark was inconsequential, something about wishing he could listen instead to the soothing lullaby of the sea, but Droikha was furious. He boorishly broke our customs by referring to Kursa's mother, a thing not done in our society.

What did he say?

Droikha said that if he wished to hear the ocean, Kursa might just listen to the sounds inside his mother's head. Kursa was stunned for a moment, then said that at least his mother's laugh didn't sound like a dog trying to throw up.

Then they came to blows?

Not yet. Droikha then said: speaking of dogs, your mother is so ugly that her dog closes his eyes when he humps her leg.

Nev paused for a swig of wine, then went on. Then Kursa said, I hear that when your daddy kisses your mama, he has to lick a horse's ass to get rid of the taste. And there was more, much more.

Did anyone laugh? I wondered.

Laugh? Certainly not, these were vile and serious breaches of conduct. One of them, I forget who, said your mama's face turned Medusa to stone, and the other said, well, your mama has so much hair on her face that it looks like she's eating a muskrat.

It went on for a long time. The last remark I remember was Droikha saying that what sounded like wolves howling at night was Kursa's mama begging wild animals to fuck her. That was the actual duel; the fight was very short.

What happened afterward?

Droikha lay unconscious for three days. He awoke from a powerful dream, a journey to the edge of death, went straight to Kursa and clobbered him, strangled him with his bare hands, drank his blood and took his skull - that's it he's drinking from now - as is our custom. That was the first man he killed, though he's killed many, women and children, too, since.

What was in the dream that makes him kill?

Who knows? But as Droikha lay near death he must have looked into the Void, as we Scyths say. I believe the Void looked back, and it posed him a question. What this question is not even he can articulate, but it's a riddle so urgent that it leaves little room in his noggin for other matters. He seeks the answer everywhere, not least in the dying faces of his victims. Apart from this riddle, his skull is an empty cup.

He certainly seems to want to kill me, I said.

And he probably will, Nev answered. Sooner or later.

I resolved to stay as close beside Nev as possible from then on. As long as he was around, I'd be reasonably safe from the Void. A week later Nev died.

He had begun by complaining of headache and thirst, then his eyes and mouth gushed blood and he lay at last thrashing in his wagon, his ulcerated skin unable to bear even the weight of Kashmir silk.

Two days before he died, though, word came that a new caravan approached, and not expecting to survive the day, I rode with Droikha and the others to our usual place of ambush. My heart sank when I saw the travellers, and fell even lower when I heard their tongue.

You remember the K'Habiru, I said to Droikha. How they were so poor they had only a single, ghostly god? Here's another sorry gaggle of them, just as ragged and funny. Remember how we laughed? Why, you can see at a glance they have nothing worth taking.

Then they have nothing much to live for, either, Droikha said.

He gave a sign to the hillside archers, drew his bow, fitted an arrow and turned to the men around us.

Kill them to hell, he said.

Afterward, some of the Scyths argued against leaving the bodies strewn across the valley to warn future prey, but in the end Droikha prevailed. The raiding season, he said, was over, and we left the K'Habiru bones to bleach along the Araxes and rode back to camp with our trophies, a string of emaciated donkeys. The prizes taken scarcely seemed to warrant the feast Droikha ordered, but the revelry served at least to drown out the dying screams of Nev. Despite my fear of wolves, I spent the night huddled in the rocks outside of camp, beyond Droikha's murderous, drunken grasp.

As soon as Nev finished dying we packed up and started north, our progress slowed by our wagons and livestock and oxcarts filled with treasure. The Indian concubines tried to follow on foot but they gradually weakened and fell behind, where the wilderness surely claimed them. Nev's corpse, covered with mounds of sedge and blue hyssop and coriander, rattled along in his own wagon. Some of the Scyths were unsteady on their mounts, stopping often to shit or suck greedily from the streams. It was now autumn. The sky was low and gray and a thin coat of snow dusted us each morning. In the winter, Scythian nomads move to higher pasture where wind sweeps away the snow so that their horses may graze. Nev was to have a proper chieftain's burial, but soon the hard earth would refuse him, and his body would travel with us until the spring thaw.

When we reached the meadow where we first met, though, the soil still yielded to our mattocks, and we began chopping out the large tomb-pit which they call a kurgan. It was hard work; now and then one of my fellow diggers collapsed with bloody eyes and was borne away to die. No one spoke of the sickness now manifest among us.

A larch tree was felled and hollowed out and carved with Nev's clan signs, and he was laid therein in his riding boots and leather breeches, red sash, bright silk shirt and a helmet of beaten gold bearing the eyes and tusks of a wild boar. The shamans had gutted him and drawn out his brains, stuffed his chest and belly with straw and herbs, replaced his eyes with scraps of felt and sewed him back together with horsehair thread. Except for the pustules on his face, he presented a noble, colorful figure.

Around him were laid his bow and axes and fighting blades and his good iron war armor, too invested with the nobility of combat for use in the past summer's banditry. Plates of gold and fine jewelry covered his body and at his feet lay his best saddles and rugs and clay pots of food to sustain his long wanderings in the valley of the happy beyond. But of more interest to me was an item missing from the heap - my chart of the world and its wonders.

After Nev's casket was carried into the pit, six horses were led down beside it and slain with axe blows to the head. He was entitled as well to six concubines. After a fierce argument over who was at fault for leaving our own girls behind, six new ones - they cannot have been older than twelve - were bought from a nearby Macronian tribe and dragged into the kurgan, wailing in terror until their throats were slit and their blood colored the earth. From this same village we obtained several large timbers which they said they had salvaged from the wreck of a mighty ship which Zeus had miraculously stranded high up on holy Mt. Theches in ancient times. To our surprise, these arrived at our meadow dragged by the two elephants we had allowed to pass some weeks earlier; they had not perished in the mountains, but been adopted and cared for by the otherwise quite vicious Macronian tribesmen. These timbers we split and shaped to make a roof above Nev's coffin and grave goods. All that remained was to mound the kurgan over with dirt and rocks, erect a stone menhir in his honor and to hold the funerary feast.

As the time neared, I considered my situation. Apart from Droikha, none of the others had ever threatened me. I was a slave, but a docile and useful one, and I moved among them freely. But I knew that Droikha meant to kill me, if not immediately then certainly over the long, idle winter. And the sickness was spreading: while we made the grave, three more of our band died and a dozen more lay on pallets from which they would never rise. The Scyths bore this with little curiosity or comment, but I sensed worse to come, and thought I knew what it was. I had read of just such symptoms in accounts of the plague that killed Pericles and decimated Athens two decades earlier, and I suspected that the girls from Byzantium had carried it to us. Even if the sickness took Droikha before he killed me, it would just as surely take me, too, in the end. To remain among this company was to die, and so I made my decision.

On the day of Nev's burial a heavy snow began to fall. His kinsmen wrapped themselves in robes of mink and musk-rat and, sobbing like children, pushed the soil in place and pounded it firm. Except for the squat menhir, actually a passable likeness of Nev, which the Macronians would likely steal once we had moved on, it would soon be an ordinary grassy hillock on which sheep, or perhaps elephants, would graze.

Bonfires were lit, cups of mare's milk and wine were poured, the gusles began to screech and quaver and the smoke of roasting oxen rose to mingle with dancing snow in a black sky. The shamans keened songs of lamentation as they tossed bundles of hemp on the fires, and soon the Scyths were staggering about in a more drunken, maudlin frenzy than any I'd witnessed.

I put on my leather breeches and long riding boots, wool tunic and cape and a cap lined with wolf's fur, stuck a dagger in my sash and made my way cautiously among the mourners, looking for Droikha.

He sat beside one of the firepits, listening as the citharode plucked his gusle and sang some tragic hero rhyme, and I knew he would not leave during this performance. In his lap he held Nev's miniature catapult, toying with it morosely. I backed away and headed for the wagons.

No Scythian would steal from the tribe, so no guard was ever posted over our common cache of plunder, but any possession of the dead not buried with them was free for the taking. I had guessed that Droikha might covet my map, and I was correct - I found it in his wagon, made sure my waterproof quiver was secure and slung it over my shoulder. In the wagons where our booty was kept, spoils as much mine as anyone's, I reasoned, since I'd materially assisting in stealing them, I filled a sack with gold coins, rings and brooches of silver and gold, and scooped in handfuls of cave pearls, lapis, amethysts and other stones. This I fixed to my sash with thongs, then crept away from the circles of firelight to the horses. I saddled my pony, tied my waterskin to the pack frame and mounted. For a few moments I sat there in the darkness, snow whispering past, gazing back at my captors reeling and dancing between the bonfires. What they would do if they caught me, I did not try to imagine.

But I was not afraid. Six months earlier I had come there as a gangling, beardless milksop. This night I was hard and brown from toil and the saddle. I had a knife at my waist, a fine mount, and I'd learned to ride from the greatest horse warriors on earth. Let them try and catch me, I thought, and in wild exultation I nudged my pony out into the storm.

Against the flux of snow I rode northwest, climbing the trail to Zagana Pass, where I huddled against my horse until first light. In the dawn we descended, carefully picking our way above the clouded ravines. In the Khorsat, the air was thick with mist and the welcome, resounding rumble of the sea grew louder. At length we came out upon the broad coastal highway and stood, stiff with ice and sweat, before the gates of Trapezus.

The gate keeper eyed me with alarm; it took a carnelian ring from Bactria to persuade him I was less dangerous than I looked. He saw first to my gallant pony, then showed me to an inn where I found a bed and fell at once into a more benumbed slumber than I had ever known, dreaming of Melisanthe and of the ship that would soon, very soon, carry me to find her.

Think, Lady Moon, how my love came to be.
Turn, Magic Wheel, and drive my lover home.

Chapter Four

Manu's Journey

I SLEPT THAT DAY AND ANOTHER NIGHT, awoke ravenous and gorged on those civilized victuals absent among the Scyths: fresh figs, honeycakes, good bread soaked in wine. After seeing to the comfort of my pony, I went to the baths, where I cleaned my teeth with boar bristles and pumice and bought a strigil to scrape the coating of barbarian grime from my body. I bought a new tunic, mantle and cloak, fastening them with a silver Luristani pin from my hoard, but my long riding boots I kept against the winter winds, apart from which I looked a proper Greek again.

There was news. Alcibiades had been recalled to Athens to face trial for the desecrations of Hermes, but not before his fleet had been destroyed off the Sicilian coast. Rather than face humiliation at home, he had fled - improbably, to Sparta - and been given refuge by his homeland's greatest enemies.

Whether or not his harim was still with him was gossip too trivial to have travelled such a distance. This turn of events troubled me, but I at least had my freedom, an ample purse, enough even to ransom Melisanthe if need be, and, after months of slavery and fear, was master of my own destiny once more. If fate willed it, I would beard the Spartans in their own harsh land - they could scarcely be more savage than the Scyths.

The city led down to the docks in a series of landings lined with tavernas, whorehouses and maritime industries, a small temple of Poseidon and a minor oracle at which Jason the Argonaut was alleged to prophesy. In a mood of confidence I made my way down to arrange passage back to the Aegean.

At the harbor, I stared out in horror. Slabs of ice floated around the hulls of the three remaining ships. The port of Trapezus was closed: no ship would arrive, nor any sail, until Spring. The Euxine, it seems, is made impassable by jagged ice floes each winter and navigation ceases until the thaw. The overland route along the coast was also out of the question, wild beasts and cannibals having infested the region since the days of Herakles, and south led straight to Droikha's band. My quest was therefore delayed for another five or six months, and I had no choice but to settle in and wait.

I took a spacious room overlooking the agora, furnished it with a bed and drafting table and replenished my ink, brushes and mapping tools. I had a balcony on which, in fine weather, I sat with my map, adding to it details I'd learned from the victims of Scythian banditry. On colder days I worked at the library of Andraeus, a magnificent new structure rising above the harbor, which also housed a school of philosophy with scholars from every race and nation. The building was finished except for the inscription on its towering facade - a windy paean large enough to be read at sea, extolling the virtues of its patron. Andraeus himself was scarcely literate, a vain, ambitious merchant wealthy from trade in grain and wine, and it was no secret that he coveted for his creation the title of Eighth Wonder. It was, however, a splendid library, with a collection of rare geographical works from which, having learned the pirate's craft from Nev, I shamelessly helped myself to many a new valley, peak and province.

Below my balcony the Gujarati followers of Pnum, only twelve of whom had survived, appeared, begging coins and bread in the market. One day I stopped to speak with them. Their leader, Manu, recognized me at once. After we had robbed them they'd met another, less merciful band, whose menacing blockade astride two elephants identified them as the headhunting Macronians of Mount Theches. Half of Manu's people were killed, he said, and all their food and pack animals stolen. On foot and starving the rest had straggled into Trapezus, destitute and stranded.

I felt sorry for them and told Manu how much I regretted my part in the ambush and theft of their god.

He smiled at this. Pnum, he confided, meant nothing to them; he and a few other minor deities had been brought along to sacrifice in just such circumstances. I squatted beside the old man to hear his story.

Thirty years ago, Manu said, a great prophet appeared among us, so wise that we laid aside Pnum and the others forever. For many years we lived in peace and happiness. Then we learned of the great assembly to begin next Spring in Smyrna. The wisest and holiest men of every nation will convene to test one another's claims to the truth, from which a single prophet will be elected, a universal spokesman for eternal, absolute wisdom. It is called the Chosen One Convention. We realized that however hard and long our pilgrimage must be, it was our sacred duty to bring the light of our own blessed prophet to mankind.

He is here with you, then?

Well, said Manu, yes and no. From time to time he indulged in a curious, rhythmic mudra of fingers and hands which seemed oddly familiar to me, though I did not at the time recognize it.

JOURNEY OF THE GUJARAT PROPHET AS TOLD BY MANU TO TIMALCUS OF LESBOS
BLACK EUXINE SEA
COLCHIS
TRAPEZUS
MT. THECHES
ZACANA PASS
CASPIAN SEA
ARAXES RIVER
ALAMUT FOREST
KARA KUM DESERT
BALKH
PERSIA
HINDU KUSH
KARA KOTUL PASS
TEHERAN
INDUS RIVER
VALLEY OF THE TIGER
OCEAN
GUJARAT

Two years ago, Manu continued, we set out, three thousand strong. We had sixty elephants, garlanded with flowers and banded with silver bells, topped with palmwood litters or crimson cupolas for the prophet and elders. There was a vast herd of livestock, two hundred wagons, a thousand camels. People from all over the province came to celebrate our departure, cheering, banging drums and cymbals, blowing horns.

I marveled at the colorful spectacle.

Yes, Manu went on. But the noise and commotion frightened the elephants. On the Gura River bridge, they panicked; there was a stampede. Many pilgrims and villagers perished, trampled or drowned, along with a dozen elephants and countless pack animals and oxen. The next week we spent in the cane fields across the river, lamenting and burning our dead.

Unfortunately the farmers had neglected to clear the fields of snakes. Each dusk the kraits slithered in among us. Many were bitten and died.

How dreadful!

Manu shrugged. Dreadful is the mysterious power of fate, he said; there is no deliverance from it, by wealth or by war, by dark sea beaten ships.

We had planned to bypass the Valley Of The Tiger but already delayed, we decided to risk it. The beasts got onto our scent at once. It took us twelve days to cross - tigers took two or three a night, a few camels as well.

We came then to the mighty Sindhu, or Indus, but the rains had come early, the river was a vast, rushing torrent. With the rains came flies and mosquitoes, and a fever arose among us, killing scores. The local tribes were cruel and predatory, constantly pilfering our food and livestock. Yet worse was to come.

I'm afraid to ask what it was, I said.

In the nearby hills, Manu continued, lurked a band of dacoits, a quasi-religious sect of stranglers and thugs. Somehow they learned of a holy man among us, and got into their heads that his touch could heal the sick. They crept into our camp one night, intent on stealing him away in order to sell his magical powers for profit. We fought, but they slashed their way to the prophet's tent and managed to hack off one of his legs and make off with it.

How terrible! Was he....

He lived, Manu said, but in great pain. We had a supply of opium and were able to give him some comfort. He wasn't very talky after that, though.

To remain there was death - we had to cross the river. Our best swimmers set out with stout ropes, but the spot we chose was ill-suited; four men were swallowed by quicksand. From a more solid bank, we tried again. Some twenty men made it halfway across before being swept away by the current. The first to reach the opposite shore was my eldest son. As he turned to signal his victory, he was attacked and eaten by a very large crocodile. A dozen more of the brutes slid into the water, waiting. Not until every one of the beasts had eaten his fill did one of us reach shore alive.

The crossing took two days. All but four of the elephants floundered and sank in the muck. Many men, women and children drowned, animals, too; wagons overturned and floated away. Two hundred of us deserted; another two hundred were too exhausted to continue. All told, only five hundred of our company survived - heat, fever, murder, wild beasts and the river had taken the rest. But the prophet lived, so we pushed on north.

Every tribe whose territory we passed through demanded payment. When we reached ancient Peshawar, though, we sold an ivory bust of Pnum's consort for enough funds to replenish our food and pack herd. There we had news of the dacoits. They'd been nabbed by angry villagers for fraud, hung up by their ankles over slow fires until their skulls roasted. The prophet's leg was recovered and given dignified immolation.

North through Punjab and Kashmir there were more bandits, always more. In some regions the cobras were especially thick, and our shepherd children were easy prey for the hyenas.

In the Kush, we knew the Uzbek slave traders were a great danger, and while we detoured to avoid them, they caught up to us as we prepared our ascent over the Kara Kotul Pass. They pierced the collarbones of two hundred of our strongest women and men, strung them together with horsehair rope and led them off to be sold in Kabul. Their villainous khan found our prophet, and, having no use for a one-legged slave, chopped off his head.

I gasped at this. I'm so sorry, Manu. I thought...1 guess I thought he was still with you.

Well, he is. In a way - but Death ate his name that day. We were in turmoil. Many gave up, took the elephants and headed back south. The rest of us felt that the wisdom we bore was too important to abandon. Reverently, we cut the prophet into pieces for transport over the pass, packed them in snow and began our climb. But the delay had cost us.

Near the summit, a blizzard swept in. Snowblind, some wandered away and fell to their deaths or were devoured by the wolves who howled around our dung fires at night. Two parcels of the divine prophet's flesh were lost on the descent, but we had enough left of him to go on.

In Balkh, we rested - a mistake. A low, miasmic valley famous for the pestilence called Balkh Fever, the water there is poisonous. Further weakened, we faced the most inhospitable region in all Asia - the vast Kara Kum Desert, a thousand stades of black sand, treeless, waterless, deserted. Heat, thirst and delirium were our enemies there. The sick perished first; men and women cut their own throats in despair and we had no choice but to abandon those who fell behind.

We pushed north into the great tamarisk forests of Alamut. At first, it was cool and lovely - then the apes appeared, vicious, taunting monsters, gibbering overhead, throwing their shit at us, stealing what they could grab. Deeper in the woods we became lost. Darkness, night and day, closed in and the trees were infested with ghouls and demons who leapt down upon us, screeching and cackling. We panicked, straggling out of the forest in small groups.

Many were disheartened and gave up. Yet we persevered, knowing that even slain and in pieces, our prophet exhibited greater wisdom than any who might contend in Smyrna. Into Armenia we marched. Finally we reached the river Araxes, east of the valley where your Scythian friends attacked us.

Hardly my friends! I interrupted. They were murderous beasts!

Indeed, said Manu. The beastheart murmurs in every man's breast. I do fervently hope your own has not been blighted by those days. But let me continue: one night, as we waited for the river to permit a crossing, a pack of rabid weasels, crazed with hunger and disease, swarmed into our camp, snapping and biting. Everyone bitten later died. But the most grievous losses were the prophet's arms and other leg, devoured on the spot or borne away by the beasts. I rescued one bit of our savior's divine flesh, and we saved his skull - this we concealed in a clay pot, which we ourselves lost fording the river. So, as you see, the profane image your Scyths stole meant nothing. We had already lost almost everything.

It must be hard for you, I said. Still, you have his teachings, his words.

It is true, Manu said, that our theology has been forced to adapt somewhat to these circumstances, and that the few of us remaining are not in perfect agreement on some points. But yes, he is still with us.

Here Manu softly tapped his chest three times.

I understand, I said. And of course I did understand: their prophet was another invisible deity now. He was there forever in their hearts, and it was that memory of him they would carry, whatever the cost, on to the Chosen One Convention in Smyrna.

The next day I took my map down to show him.

I wondered, I said, when you left Gujarat, why go north? Going directly west would have been much shorter.

Manu smiled. Oh, no, Timalcus - that way is much too dangerous.

Scouts came in to report an approaching band of Scythians. Certain it was Droikha's tribe, I asked to address the archons of the city. The Scyths were occasional visitors there; they came to trade and never made any trouble, but my description of the plague they carried changed everything, and it was voted to bar their entry. Trapezus had heavy gates and thick walls, manned by militia. We would be safe within, for I knew the Scyths were raiders, not layers of siege.

When they arrived at the gates they were at first indignant, denying any sickness among them. At length they confessed their condition and asked for doctors or medicine, neither of which were judged safe to grant them. But they did not depart then as I'd expected; they camped in the hills and helped themselves to the crops and livestock outside our walls. I had stabled my pony there, the gentle beast to whom I owed my life. The Scyths reclaimed her, and I never saw her again.

As a frequent visitor to the library, over time I became acquainted with some of the scholars in residence, in particular with Kasperius the Cynic and Polyxo the Theist, two brilliant, articulate men whose views on nearly every subject could scarcely have been more opposite. Both found me a willing listener, and both sought to convert me. When I dined with Polyxo, Kasperius often joined us, mocking religion with a vehemence that might have gotten him arrested in Athens. Polyxo, when he heard I was conversing with Kasperius, would come running to defend - as he saw it - my tender young mind from corruption. I found them both hugely entertaining.

Polyxo tried to convince me that the gods and goddesses were real and therefore deserved our devotion. The universe exists, he argued, therefore, like everything that exists, some agency must have created it. This agency must of necessity be older and greater than the universe it created.

Nonsense, scoffed Kasperius. If everything that exists requires a creative agency, then the gods, if they exist, require a creator as well. And that creator necessitates an even greater creator, who requires another, and so on to absurd infinity.

I have often wondered about this, I said. The Orphics begin with Eurynome, Mother of All Things, but give her no parents. Even Hesiod takes us back no further than Darkness and Chaos.

Both scholars smiled at me.

We have before us a budding philosopher, said Kasperius. The boy has a mind and some education.

I had been caught showing off, and I blushed.

Indeed, Polyxo said. But see here: First Cause is an exception by paradox. Since we cannot logically deny the existence of paradox, and we can neither explain nor ignore it, we must, ad interum, take it at face value, as a thing beyond or outside of mere logic.

My dear fellow, Kasperius responded, you propose logically embracing illogic. The true nature of paradox is that of dead end, an obstacle from which one can only judiciously retreat.

Polyxo ignored him. And there are many other proofs that the gods exist, he said. Mark how they reward the faithful and punish the impious. Boetius, for example, was stingy in sacrifice; he lost his wife, his fortune and his reputation.

Blame the Erinyes if you will, said Kasperius. I happen to know that his wife's lover engineered his downfall.

And noble Aristides, who prayed daily and gave generously to the temples, saw his lands prosper and his wealth increase ninefold.

Proving, said Kasperius, that Zeus will indeed smile on a man who marries well.

Deny if you can what we see with our own eyes. We've both known men who, after years of idleness and dissolute behavior, turned at last to the gods, whereupon their lives miraculously changed for the better. The power to make such profound changes in men can only be divine.

Again, Kasperius said, you see white, I see black. You see miracles and I see human nature. Men may indeed change radically, but the force at work isn't the power of the gods, it's the *belief* in the power of the gods. Some men exercise this mental gymnastic called faith to their own benefit and thus transform themselves, and insofar as drunkards, thieves and stranglers are reformed by it, civilization benefits as well. I merely observe that reason can perform the same function, and it does so without recourse to credulous fantasy.

It is no fantasy to discover in the reformed debauchee a quality he did not previously possess: virtue. And since virtue is demonstrably not innate in man, its source can only be the gods.

Ah, yes! The virtuous gods, said Kasperius. Who, according to every tradition, get drunk and fornicate and disguise themselves as drakes or stallions to diddle our womenfolk. Gods who cheat, lie and quarrel, who incessantly meddle in our affairs out of favoritism, malice, grudge and boredom. What rubbish! And if virtue is exclusively divine, it follows that an old atheist like me is incapable of it.

He rose from the table, withdrew an obol from his purse, gave it to a beggar and rejoined us with a smirk.

Divine Hestia made you do that, Polyxo said.

And so it went with them, day after day.

The archons interrupted my studies one morning. Since I knew something of the Scythians, they wished my opinion of a curious new development outside the gates. We went to the upper city, climbed the wall and peered out over the parapet.

Droikha's men were gathered in the pasture below. They had cut timber in the hills, dragged it down with oxen and were busy shaping and notching the boles. Some staggered weakly.

Can you tell us what they're up to?

I studied the Scyths for a moment.

They're building a catapult, I said. To knock down your walls.

The archons laughed. One slapped the thick stone ramparts. Not these walls, he said, not in a thousand years.

I wasn't worried. Nev might have made it work, but not crazy Droikha.

Kasperius, Polyxo and I began to meet every day for our midday meal in a taverna near the library, neither of them willing to allow the other time with me alone. I asked them one day about the Chosen One Convention. They were well informed about it, both in fact planning to attend and observe if they could afford it. It was to begin in the spring and was expected to last a year or more.

Kasperius explained that the concept originated among the K'Habiru tribes of Syria and Jebu-Ur-Salim. From time to time, they believed, a chosen, or anointed one called a Mashaiya would appear among mankind as a divine messenger, whose mission was to unite men in wisdom. Other races had similar expectations: Hindus awaited a new Krishna, Buddhists the Maitreya. And many other old cultures believed that new deities would appear or beloved dead ones return to life - Greek Dionysus, Phrygian Attis, Nilotic Osiris and so on.

Polyxo, here, Kasperius said, will argue that such a source of wisdom and virtue already exists, in the Greek pantheon and its rites, and that no new savior is needed.

And you'll argue....

That the whole idea is superstitious claptrap. We must use our own minds rather than rely on cowled, babbling, moon-blind priests with their obsolete and incomprehensible dogma.

Dogma which most men accept, said Polyxo. You're in a very small minority, you know.

Kasperius snorted in contempt. Truth isn't decided by a vote, he said, but by logic. And most of what passes for logic consists of men adopting arguments supporting propositions which they've already decided to believe.

I have personally witnessed divine power, said Polyxo. As I cannot possibly perceive what does not exist, it follows that what I do perceive *must* exist. Therefore, my belief is not only logical, it is an apodictic modality - it is true because it cannot be false.

Kasperius was visibly amused. Leaving aside the obvious flaws in your argument, he said, such as imperfect perception, allow me to follow your proposition further to a favorite proposition of my own. Having established this belief to your own not terribly demanding standards, you have reached a conclusion - that the gods do in fact exist. But what is the nature of conclusion? It's the point at which the matter requires no additional thought, the point at which your mind is irrevocably closed on the subject. It's the point where you got tired of thinking. You abandon critical consideration and claim to *know.*

I do know....

You know nothing, Polyxo. Nor, I hasten to add, do I. To claim the final word on any question is lazy, wishful thinking, self-delusion and, I might add, in its smug claim of infallibility, breathtaking arrogance.

Kasperius, I protested, you come very close to insult. You may disagree with Polyxo, but surely we must respect the beliefs of others.

Rubbish, said Kasperius. Respect a patently foolish idea? What we must respect, for good or ill, is another man's absolute right to hold some idiotic notion different from our own.

Despite their differences, they had something in common - they had both become fond of me, and I came to trust their discretion and good will.

One day I confessed to them my crime against the crow god and my fear that his wrath pursued me.

After Polyxo instructed me on how to expiate my sin, I turned to Kasperius for his usual mockery. To my surprise, he took the matter seriously.

You've made a dangerous enemy, he said.

But you don't even believe Cronus really exists, I pointed out.

He doesn't, but that makes him no less dangerous.

I wondered how this could be so.

It's true, Kasperius said, that the gods don't exist outside our imaginations, but within those fantasies we endow them with a rich multiplicity of traits - quirks and motives which keep us always guessing. Today we imagine they smile on us, tomorrow their displeasure may loosen our anus holes in terror. We give insufficient thought to the consequences of the natures we assign them.

The current ruling deities are, to be sure, less than ideal, but old Cronus is infinitely more savage and primitive than they. His totem, the crow, is the most clever of winged creatures and also the cruelest, an omnivorous trickster and thief. He will gang with his tribe to mob other birds' nests and devour their young, then steal and hide food from his own family. He will pluck the eyes from a helpless newborn lamb and cackle wickedly about it. He delights in taunting dogs and cats and humans....

This I've seen, I said.

Just so, Kasperius went on, Cronus in his prime was cunning and cruel enough to gobble up his own children. Now, overthrown by his ungrateful brats, cast into hell, deprived of power and dignity, he is forced to watch his buffoon son bask in our homage. Other gods will come and go - Zeus, too, will pass - but Cronus will never again be in vogue. He knows us humans, rightly, as fawning but fickle dogs. Yet he lacks one perspective that is ours: the restful embrace of death, a blessing surely earned by used-up men, is a release denied the gods. The crow god's harshest fate is the tedium of eternity. Cronus knows immortality for the farce and travesty it is. No wonder he's cranky.

My point is, Timalcus, that making the gods real gives them power over you. A bitter, primeval god like Cronus can intrude between your persona and the civilized, rational man you aspire to be. Even half believing in him might turn you into his murderous acolyte. Only reason can free you.

Ritual, said Polyxo. Faith and ritual.

Reason.

No, faith.

Waiting for my friends one morning outside the library, I admired the broad curve of its towering entry. Workers hoisted tiles, each a handsomely crafted Greek letter, up to masons who were cementing them in place. The dedication, still unfinished, began with a genealogy of Andraeus and his wife and went on to describe their virtues and honors. Idly, I began to read it and was soon shaking with laughter.

The foreman saw me and came running, redfaced and angry at my insult.

But can't you see? Look, I said, there, instead of Andraeus you've got Antheus - 'flower-sissy' instead of 'manly man.'

Below that, it implies that he's a hermaphrodite. Some of the letters are sideways, a few upside down. The description of his wife seems to mention either barley or drunken apes. The whole thing is ludicrous.

Polyxo and Kasperius came out just then. They had noticed the errors but said nothing, as Andraeus was their patron. My bringing the problems to light was a great relief to them.

That afternoon Andraeus's secretary came to my lodgings. My scholar friends had recommended me to take on the task of overseeing the inscription's correction and completion. I gladly accepted, not just for the generous salary offered, but for something to occupy my months of waiting.

With plague-ridden Scyths at the gates and the sea closed to us, food and water began to grow scarce in the city. The warehouses of Andraeus, however, held thousands of amphorae of wine, which he generously distributed among the Trapezans. But proper Greeks drink their wine well blended with water - only barbarians guzzle it straight, so the townsfolk began increasingly to attend their daily routines stumbling about in vinous jocularity. Thus, when the Scythians seemed ready to test their hurling machine, the mob that gathered on the walls to watch were merry and festive with drink.

Droikha's men canted the contraption, wound its cable tight and rolled a large stone into the sling.

The lever was thrown, the bowstring quivered and snapped; timbers splintered and the projectile toppled comically to earth, crushing one unlucky fellow's leg.

Trapezus howled with laughter and its inhabitants returned boisterously to their affairs.

I discovered that the problem with the library inscription was that while many of the men were skilled craftsmen, they were no more literate than goats. The letters meant nothing to them. My first reform, therefore, was to introduce an alphabet class each morning, and after a few days most of them could bring on my command a xi or alpha or mu from the stacks. But the function of these strange symbols still eluded them. I hit on the method of asking each his name, then sending him for the requisite letters, which I then laid out in the correct order on the flagstones.

The exercise proved enormously popular; they were avid to see their identities so expressed and repeated it again and again. Soon the better students were proudly laying out their names when they arrived each morning, and showing them to passersby.

Then I made a terrible mistake. Laptes had arranged his name on the horizontal, and I decided to show off a bit. I sent Hypus for his tiles and when he returned, had him discard the pi, at which he fretted anxiously lest I should somehow dishonor his persona. All of the men gathered around, watching in silence as I laid out the tiles like this:

$$
\begin{array}{c}
H \\
Y \\
L\,A\ \ P\ T\ E\ S \\
U \\
S
\end{array}
$$

I rose smiling from my creation. Can you see what I've done? I asked. You can take the letters and arrange them....

The workmen stared uneasily at the conjoined names.

What's wrong?

There was a long silence. Finally one of them spoke.

We don't like it, he said.

They went slowly back to their work. After that, many of them avoided my gaze, and I sometimes turned to find them staring curiously at me. When I came near, their conversation ceased. Annoyed, I left the two names where they lay; the men would not go near them, but the next morning they had vanished, and no one could say where they had gone.

The midwinter festival was celebrated with an abundance of wine but no feasting. All the fresh food had been consumed, but the city granaries held sufficient barley for our bread and enough wheat and oats to stew into sour virpa mash. If spring came on time no one would starve.

The two philosophers and I often lingered at table on cold days. Polyxo continued to urge me to pay respects to the gods.

Tradition is important, he said. Men have always believed in the deities; it is our cultural heritage to do so.

We also used to believe that a man's jism was stored in his head, said Kasperius, and that eating beans made women pregnant. Shall we cling to such superstitions out of tradition? No, my friend, belief is a process, not a constant. What we're certain of today will seem ridiculous tomorrow.

All the great thinkers and poets, Homer included, honored these traditions, Polyxo argued. They wrote of the gods as real and consequential.

Yes, by all means, Kasperius answered, let's substitute liter-ature for science and myth for physics and medicine. Any fool can write a book.

True enough. And by the way, how is your book coming along?

Even Kasperius laughed at this.

There was a commotion in the streets; people were rushing to the upper city to watch a second comical attempt at bom-bardment by the hapless Scyths, and we joined them.

The catapult had been overhauled, timbers reinforced, a smooth notch chiseled in the pointing beam - it was now a nearly perfect copy of the design I had seen and replicated in miniature. The Scythians cranked the sling taut and loaded it. The citizens of Trapezus tittered in tipsy anticipation.

Then we took an involuntary step back, watching in horror as the mighty stone soared into the sky, arced above the wall on which we stood and smashed through the roof of a sandal-maker's shop behind us.

Droikha's band began to jeer wildly at us. They broke out their jugs of wine and mare's milk and cuffed each other about in congratulations. Tonight, I guessed, they would drink and celebrate; tomorrow the assault would begin in earnest. The chastened crowd went silently back to their occupations, and I was not alone in glancing back for a reassuring look at the massive walls.

In a pensive mood I returned to the library, where a new problem had now arisen. Letter tiles were disappearing from the site, apparently pilfered from the stacks at night. I chose a man I trusted and set him to guard the premises from dusk to dawn.

The next morning a thin, wintry mist hung over the pasture where the Scyths reset their engine and cranked its cables tight. Most of the Trapezans had come to watch, shivering in the chill air. The besiegers fitted a missile into its sling.

That's not a stone, said Polyxo. It's a man.

The sling snapped smartly and a human form was launched into the fog. He sailed gracefully over the ramparts and landed with a horrifying crunch of bone and flesh in the square. We gathered around the corpse.

One of the archons prodded me: See if you know him.

I crept closer, noting the man's long, fair braids and the pool of blood spreading from his cracked skull. He lay on his back, limbs splayed, motionless. When I stood over him I knew, despite his mottled mask of pox, that it was my nemesis, Droikha the Void. I knelt beside him, filled with unexpected pity.

Poor Droikha, I said. I bear you no....

His bloodrimmed eyes flickered open and his hands shot forth to seize my neck.

I'll kill you to hell, he croaked.

Soldiers ran to help me. Unable to dislodge Droikha's iron grip, they drew their swords and hacked at his arms. I found myself abruptly freed, and staggered away, his rough fingers still around my throat, his severed forearms flailing at my chest. Slowly his grip relaxed and his hands were pried away. Gasping, I stood above Droikha and looked down at him.

He lay writhing, blood spurting rhythmically from the open sockets of his elbows, red foam from his lips darkening his beard. His movements subsided, his eyes widened and he stared up at the sky with a look of astonishment.

Rosebud! he cried. It's rosebud!

Then he finished dying.

Droikha, it seemed, had finally found the answer to that terrible question posed to him so long ago at the edge of the void, but it did not strike me as an answer likely to be of much use to anyone else.

When the second Scythian warrior hurled into the city - he appeared to have died a day or two previously - was also seen to be infected, the immediate aim of the attackers became frighteningly clear, though precisely what they hoped to achieve by foisting the plague upon Trapezus was not. We had no way, however, to prevent them from the attempt. Rewinding the catapult's sling was a lengthy process, many of the Scyths seemed weak and slow, so, on a good day they could manage no more than eight or nine launches. They had occasional misfires, too, when the human projectiles splatted harmlessly against our battlements. Of those clearing the walls, most were already dead or died on impact; a few lived an hour or two, moaning and cursing in the street or on a rooftop, and the militia was delegated to carry them away. I urged the archons to have them burned, but this violated some city ordinance, so the mangled, poxfilthy bodies of flying nomad horsemen laid in open pits for days on end. It took only a week for sickness to break out among the soldiers, upon which they refused further duty, and after that the dead Scyths remained where they fell.

By the last month of winter plague had spread throughout the town. A woman crazed with fever went mad and threw herself down the city's only undepleted well, poisoning our last source of water. People fought over rainwater and the handfuls of snow that fell - apart from this meager supply, there was only wine to drink.

Shops closed and commerce ceased. Men and women staggered about, drunk or sick, or both. They wandered, sleepless and convulsing and vomiting bile; their fingers and noses and ears turned black and fell off; they howled and stripped themselves naked and fell dead in the streets where they lay until roaming packs of dogs devoured them. Sick and dying children and aged parents were turned out, doors barred against their feeble cries. Surly with wine and misery, men quarreled and killed one another in brawls, and sought out young girls to rape. And bloodmottled corpses fell endlessly from the sky.

But in the harbor of Trapezus the ice began to melt, the breezes promised rain and the Scythian horde was dwindling: their barrage must surely cease before long, if for no other reason than lack of ammunition.

The plague had devastated the city. Only a few of those infected survived, but Polyxo was one of them. His fellow scholars nursed him and he recovered with no worse effects than hair loss and a ragged blazon of pox scars across his jowls. Kasperius and I seemed immune, as did Manu, though his clan of Dactylists, as they now called themselves, had been reduced to only eight of the three thousand pilgrims who'd left Gujarat.

Dactylic lore, a subcult of the ancient Orphic Mysteries, is the art of finger augury and symbolism practiced by the Pelasgians who inhabited Greece before the Hellenes arrived. How these wanderers from India came to adopt it I couldn't guess. When I asked Manu he only held up his hand and wagged a finger at me with a mischievous smile. But I had no time then to ponder his arcane religious nonsense - matters at the library had become critical.

Half my workmen failed to report each day; I presumed them sick, perhaps dead. Moreover, my letter tiles continued to vanish at an alarming rate, and my watchman claimed to have seen nothing. Due to the shortage of letters I was forced to revise the dedication radically, deleting the lesser of Andraeus's honors and ancestors. It was not, I thought privately, a great loss to literature. Still, I was annoyed, and I decided to stand guard myself. I told no one of my plan.

They came in the darkest hour, six of them, and as I'd guessed, my guard let them pass. With a whispered consultation they selected a few tiles, wrapped them in their cloaks and slithered away into the night.

I was angry. Certain that they were black marketeers who were selling the expensive tiles for profit, I followed. On the portico of a hall where masons and other craftsmen met and lodged, they were greeted in hushed secrecy. I crept after them through the dark interior to a shaft of light rising from the cellar. On the landing, I crouched and peered down.

Two dozen men, most of whom I recognized, moved about the torchlit chamber. On the floor they had laid out hundreds of tiles spelling out their names and the names of deities, and other words and letters, all in an intricate, interwoven pattern which nearly filled the room. As I tried to make sense of this, they prowled among this mosaic with a somber cadence of prayer and incantation, placing new tiles into the maze with great ceremony, consecrating the letters with libations of wine.

Their creation looked like this:

The whole thing made my flesh crawl. What black, uncanny arts, what traffic with demons these mad fools pursued was beyond my ken, and nothing could have induced me to beard this cult in their secret labyrinth of pilfered script. I backed quietly away into the darkness; Eighth Wonder of the World or not, the Library of Andraeus would just have to suffer.

In the month of Thargelion enough rain fell to replenish the city's wells, buds sprouted on the trees, ice turned again to brine in the harbor and those corpses spared the fate of canine fodder played hosts to feasting newborn maggots. Fewer than twenty Scythians remained at our gates, managing only a few desultory cadaver flingings a week, but the plague had run its course; no new infections were reported, and the surviving populace, dazed, weak and astonished to be alive, slowly returned to their trades and pursuits.

Three vessels stood at anchor in the port. Their owners had been dined and courted and plied with bribes and gifts all winter long by the city's richest men, and they were at last ready to open bidding on their services. Tables for the negotiations were set up in the Council House, where noble men with embroidered silk mantles and fat purses lined up to secure passage for themselves and their families from the hell of Trapezus. I took my library wages and my sack of purloined gems and stood among them, regarded with amused contempt by Andraeus and the others, but when my turn came I went boldly before the shipowners and their captains and poured out my heap of coins and jewelry and precious stones.

I wish to book passage to Smyrna, I said, for myself, my two scholar friends and the Gujarati pilgrims, eight in number, making eleven in all.

My rivals had gold and silver coins, and could offer wine and amber and furs, but none, not even Andraeus, had such a cache of immediately negotiable treasure. In liquid assets, I was the richest man in Trapezus.

I discovered then that I possessed a good many bosom friends of whom I'd previously been unaware. I brushed them aside and took my time in selecting my ship, a sleek merchant caravel providing comfortable quarters and a swifter journey. The others gaped at me in hatred as I strode out, but their envy meant nothing to me, for I had outlasted the malice of the Fates. Once again I controlled my own destiny, and only my own failure of nerve and determination stood between me and my beloved, a failure no longer possible, for I was not the callow boy who'd left Lesbos: I was almost seventeen.

Kasperius and Polyxo were grateful and touched, thanking me endlessly, but in truth I'd become so fond of them that I never thought of leaving them behind. Manu's people were ecstatic - the girl, Chitra, garlanded me with flowers; her father tried to kiss my feet, until in embarrassment I shooed them away.

At the library I assembled my men, sending some to fetch absentees I knew were alive and well. They came trickling in, some shamefaced, others defiant. When they were all present, I addressed them.

I know who has been stealing the letters, I said, and I know what you've been doing with them.

The guilty men stirred uneasily.

But we have only the final section of the dedication left, and I would like to see it finished before I go. If you will cease your thefts for the time being and pitch in to complete the work, I will not inform the archons, or Andraeus, of your crimes. And what happens to any tiles that may be left over will not concern me.

They were getting off lightly - Andraeus, as they well knew, could have had them exiled, even executed in some horrible fashion. It didn't take them long to agree to my terms.

We had completed, as best we could, Andraeus's honors and genealogy. I turned my attention to the remaining text, and after taking inventory of the remaining tiles, I saw that these last lines must be trimmed. As I set about this redaction, my crew went back to work with new energy and enthusiasm.

From our passage funds I had retained a few coins and smaller gems for our expenses. At Polyxo's urging, I left a token offering to Poseidon, asking, as seafarers will, for a safe voyage. He also pressed me to consult the oracle, which Kasperius, of course, thought a waste of money.

A whore is better value, he said.

I told him about Orpheus's words on Lesbos. What had then seemed gibberish about pestilence, Icarus and stolen words now seemed prescient, though little good it had done me. In the end, as the Oracle of Jason the Mariner was nearby and not very expensive, I decided to give it a try.

Knowing better what to expect this time, I took jugs of wine and water and some coins to the shrine, a modest temple tucked among warehouses and sail-menders' shops above the harbor. The priest took my obols; we performed our ablutions and he led me straightaway into the antron. The sibyl tottered out, her sallow flesh slack from our recent near famine, seated herself and began to munch on a cud of laurel leaves. Presently she spoke:

The gods pen their rhymes in the blood of human endeavor;
The voltas they write grind dust and bones like machines of war.
Their ink eats through the parchment, for into their milk is bile.
The tongueless wanderer signs his loss with madness,
And your traveller's skin is a skein of scrolls
Upon which unroll all possible griefs.

The priest followed me to the entrance and without demanding further payment began a courteous reading.

The Great Mariner, he said, bids you exercise caution at sea. Where your journey leads near the clash of war, stay well clear. And neither tempt nor annoy the gods more than necessary.

Bland and useless platitudes, I thought, just as Kasperius predicted. That last line, I said - what's this business about grief?

He placed a hand on my shoulder and gave me a gentle smile. Sorrow, he said, is the human condition, my son. Never imagine that the gods will grow weary of your tears, even in death.

As dawn broke over the mountains of Colchis, an envious crowd watched us board our ship. The crew bustled about and my friends and I, prosperous tourists at leisure, stood on deck, viewing the activity with pleasure and anticipation. Kasperius asked me about the oracle.

You were right, I told him. An old woman's insipid warnings, banal advice larded with the usual incoherent babble.

Those sibyls never last long, he said. Shut up in their gloomy caves, alternately pampered and bullied, stuffed with sweets, forcefed intoxicating mushrooms and herbs and soma, constantly gassed with those sickly vapors. They're all quite mad, you know - sooner or later.

It seems so. I'm done with such things for good.

We cast off in a stiff breeze that snapped the halyards and bellied out the canvas, tacking out of port with black water whispering past our hull. I looked back with pride at the library. From the harbor's mouth the dedication was bold and clearly visible, including the final stanza my crew had cemented into place only the day before:

ANDRAEUS III WELCOMES YOU AND DECLARES
THIS LIBRARY IS MY ERECTION -
IT IS IMMENSE - WELL ENDOWED - MADE OF
STONE AND LONG LASTING.
WITHIN, IT IS SWOLLEN WITH UNIVERSAL
KNOWLEDGE.
BY MY OWN HAND IT STANDS READY
TO DISCHARGE ITS MARVELOUS CONTENTS
UPON ALL HUMANITY.
- ANDRAEUS III OF CORINTH –

When I pointed it out, Kasperius and Polyxo said nothing directly about it, but I could tell by their broad smiles that they were proud of me and my achievement.

Think, Lady Moon, how my love came to be.
Turn, Magic Wheel, and drive my lover home.

Chapter Five

Theology Explained

A MORE MISERABLE COMPANY OF STRANDED WAYFAR-
ERS than my friends and I as we huddled outside the gates of
Heraklea Pontika can scarcely be imagined. On making port we
had gone into the city, at Polyxo's insistence, to lay an offering before the shrine of the city's patron, Herakles Lionclad.
We returned to the harbor to find our ship making ready to
sail; with gaff and dagger the crew prevented us from board-
ing. They sailed away, jeering at us, to trade, we supposed, for
amber and furs on the northern Euxine, or perhaps back to
Trapezus for more refugees to rob and abandon.

My comrades, expecting to reach Smyrna by sea in a few
days, now faced a journey of more than three thousand stades
west to Ilium, then down the coast, with few resources to sustain them. As for me, I'd had no clearer plan on reaching the
Aegean than to search for Melisanthe by tracking Alcibiades,
who was still in Sparta so far as I then knew. But there was
fresh news of him, and of the war.

Alcibiades had seduced the wife of a Spartan general and
fled again, this time to the Persian court at Sardis. During my
months with the Scyths and at Trapezus the war had gone
badly for Athens, some of their unwilling allies, including my

own Lesbos, having defected. In Athens a few hundred oligarchs had seized power for a time, and when democracy was restored the new assembly turned to an unlikely savior of their cause: Alcibiades. They'd forgiven his many treasons, absolved him of his heresies and given him an army and a fleet with which he'd lately ravaged the coast of Thrace. He marched now somewhere along the shores of Asia Minor, engaging the Spartan allies in Mysia.

For the many pilgrims and seekers and cults, with their prophets and would-be Chosen Ones and Mashaiyas bound south for Smyrna, it was terrible news that war lay in their path. But it brought my quarry much closer; once we reached the Troad, Alcibiades, perhaps with Melisanthe in his harim, was before me, only a few weeks distant. I resolved therefore to remain with my friends and travel overland to Smyrna.

Except what we wore and carried with us, all our belongings had been on the ship. Manu, Polyxo and Kasperius had between them some twenty drachmas. My map nestled in the quiver habitually slung from my shoulder, and I had a few coins and a last gemstone - a Persian turquoise I'd kept because its sparkling green hue reminded me of Melisanthe's eyes.

This I traded for six Bactrian camels and the six boys bound to the animals for life. Arabian camels would not do, Manu said; Bactrians can carry a heavier load than a wagon and break down less often, are capable of one hundred stades a day without rest and last two weeks without water. But, he cautioned me, all camels hate mankind. Once up, they obey, but will not willingly stand; I watched in horror as the boys savagely beat them where they lay, bellowing, spitting, farting and snapping. I scolded the boys for their cruelty, but within a week I, too, came to despise the vile, filthy, obstinate beasts.

In the market, Manu's expertise from his own long journey proved invaluable, though I argued stubbornly over the price of the rugs he selected. They were woven in Konya, ancient birth-place of the art of weaving, tightly spun and durable, and in the end, he wore me down. Most of our remaining funds went to provision our party with secondhand cloaks, water bags, sacks of oats for us and of barley for the camels, cooking pots, oil, dried figs, olives, ghee and honey paste, a few spoons.

On a plain outside the city, companies of merchants and bands of pilgrims were gathered. We joined them and settled in to await the assembly of sufficient numbers to make up a caravan. On our last night at Heraklea I sat talking with Kasperius and Polyxo.

Sokrates, Kasperius remarked, must have been ever so happy when the Four Hundred - the aristocrats - ruled Attica.

Probably, I said. He is no great fan of democracy.

If you parse him closely, he hints that a single wise man is the optimal form of government, though he insists he is not that man. But that's what he's after, all right, the sly old rascal - to govern Athens himself in the Spartan style he so admires. Yet the Spartans, for all their vaunted courage, are mindless sheep. Respect for a state's authority must arise from dispensation of real justice, not from thrashing blind obedience into automatons.

For once, Polyxo said, we nearly agree.

Kasperius turned to him with a harsh smile.

How then defend blind obedience to gods who are manifestly unjust?

The gods, said Polyxo, are by definition just. They may work in mysterious ways which our limited human intelligence fails to comprehend, but if we do them the required homage, if we trust them, they will, as they promise, deliver us.

Feh! said Kasperius. Pure rationalization. You understand them well enough when their actions suit you, but let them fail us and you impute to them motives majestic and recondite beyond our grasp, then say it's blasphemy to question. And deliver us from what? I don't see them protecting us from our own stupidity.

Just so, Polyxo said. Our stubborn stupidity in ignoring the directives of the gods causes all our problems.

All? See here, are these heavenly bigshots running things or not?

They are. At least those things we humans don't muck up.

All right, said Kasperius. I'll grant you war and rape and slavery are largely man's doing, that even disease thrives to some degree on our ignorance. And I'll further concede the blessings of sun and sea and barley. But who stirs up the envy and grudges that lead to war? Ares and Athene, that's who. Who carelessly incinerates our crops? By your theology, Helios. What sky god lards his rain with bolts of lightning? And doesn't Poseidon shake the earth and batter us with tidal wave and typhoon as well as fill our nets with fluke and mackerel? Don't waste our time making excuses for them. If they insist on taking credit for the bounty, they must in fairness accept blame for the destruction, too. Your gods are careless children; they toss us about like cheap toys, yet expect - no, demand - unconditional love.

I only know that without the gods' blessings I would not have survived the plague.

Well, that's another thing that just puckers my bunghole, you sanctimonious ass. Don't your fellow scholars, who nursed you at some risk to themselves, deserve a bit of credit?

I had faith the gods would guide them in caring for me.

That's right, said Kasperius. Let men do you a service, but praise the gods for it. Let others gather food, cook it and serve you, and you thank Cybele for the supper. You religious types are all alike, oblivious to human kindness while you curry favor in the clouds. Are your friends invisible? Thank *them*!

I do thank you, or rather what is best in you. And what is good and decent within you comes from above, whether you know it or not. My faith, a concept which you clearly cannot grasp, encompasses both the divine gods and their divine nature within those who serve them.

Faith? Oh, I know what faith is. A reasoning man, when hungry, seeks out something he recognizes as food. Substitute faith for logic and you'll pick up the nearest object at hand, pop it in your mouth and trust the gods to make it edible. In every other sphere of life, save this nebulous matter of religion, reason works best. Therefore I see no cause to suspend it here.

Yes, Polyxo said, reason is good, one of the gods' finer gifts to us. But reason alone cannot prove some things, including the axiom that reason is the best, or only, way to apprehend truth. And since reason is a human act, it's by definition limited and fallible, yet you stake your very soul on it. Therefore, your claim to abjure faith is false: you have faith in reason.

I have no such thing, said Kasperius. Faith is absolute, a quality I've never attributed to reason. Reason brings us only to the present moment, at which we render only our present judgment, admitting as we do so that we might be, as we've certainly been before, mistaken. To have erred, as all men have, is to possess the capacity to err again, on any matter, at any time. Admit this and you admit that every answer, every belief, is tentative - nothing more that one's best current hypothesis. So at bottom, every honest man is agnostic; he must confess he does not *know*. Religion rests on an exactly opposite notion - that final, universal answers do exist and may be perceived. If this were true, the failure to find such answers would indeed be tragic; their absence would be a dreadful void, that void which faith purports to fill. The existence of a question, however, does not necessitate the existence of its answer. This void is as imaginary as the implausible and unnecessary myths deployed to feed it.

And so you end up, Polyxo said, with abiding faith that you know nothing and never can, the paradox of being certain that you can never be certain. There's your faith, Kasperius. It differs from mine only in patience. Where you give up, I go on to reason in a different mode, open not only to mere logic, but to every nuance, every divine clue the universe offers.

So now I'm just lazy, eh? Another way to see it is that you're just too cowardly to face the truth of your own ultimate ignorance.

Polyxo gazed sadly at him for a moment.

It feels very good to know something, Kasperius. You should try it sometime. He rose then and politely excused himself from our company.

Superstitious yokel, Kasperius muttered. Self-righteous, irrational fool.

Their bickering had often before been heated, but it had remained civil. That night Kasperius's words took on a nasty edge, and I felt embarrassed for them. Afterward, I slept badly, troubled by dreams of crows and dying soldiers and of Melisanthe crying out to me. We rose before dawn and moved slowly out, southwest across the plains of Bithynia.

The caravan was large, and moved more slowly than anticipated. After four weeks we passed the Propontis and reached the ruins of windy Ilium, where Hektor died a thousand years before, and where the mound said to be the grave of Achilles still stood. The two scholars rode camels, as did Manu, whose frail, bony frame jolted along with no sign of fatigue. Now on our right the blue Aegean probed the shore, its boom or murmur never far away. Each day was much the same - we plodded dawn to dusk, eighty stades on a good day, then gathered wood for our fires and wearily boiled our virpa or plucked marsh roots to stew samphire. The aroma of kid or poultry roasting on the fires of our wealthier travelling companions tormented us, so on days when the caravan moved slowly, I took Haqim, leader of the camel boys, hunting in the spurge and seagrass of the coastal dunes. Once we snared a pheasant, twice we netted hares. These were the only meats, save one, that we tasted on the journey.

We came thus into Mysia, where those towns unfaithful to Athens lay in rubble. We began to meet deserters, wounded soldiers and other refugees straggling north - Alcibiades had ravaged the coast, and as I gazed across the straits at Lesbos, I wondered how my family had fared, and what might be left of Mytilene.

One night the remaining seven Dactylists of Manu's tribe came to me. As I had rescued them from Trapezus they considered me in some way their protector, and they sought my help.

Manu, they said, was a worthy man, but ancient. He would doubtless grow more feeble, yet he insisted on being the sole conveyor of their prophet. This holy burden, they argued, would be safer with one of the younger members.

Manu's endurance seemed excellent to me, but I saw their point - if he should die without passing on that precious wisdom which they believed he bore, it would be irrevocably lost and their journey in vain. I agreed to speak with him.

Manu, I said, your clan has asked me....

Heretics, he said.

But perhaps it's time to share the prophet's message so that all of you can carry it, in your hearts, on to Smyrna.

He looked at me intently for a moment.

You do not understand, he said.

With trembling hands he reached inside his tunic and withdrew a small pouch. Inside it was a parcel wrapped in soft Kashmir silk. Reverently he unfolded it before me.

It was a shriveled finger.

Behold, he said. The Prophet.

Tenderly, he folded it away again beside his heart, tapping it three times.

In this bit of flesh, he said, the Digit Divine, resides the last, best hope of man's spiritual redemption. Surely you see now that it cannot be further divided.

Of course, it's a finger, said the other Dactylists when I returned to their fire. What did you think it was? That's what 'dactyl' means.

Chitra took my arm.

Old Manu has lost his way, she said. He believes it to be the Fool's Finger of Epimedes, while anyone with eyes can see it's the masculine right-hand Psychic Fourth Dactyl.

Her father interrupted: Don't listen to Chitra. Foolish girl! What Manu bears is the small left Sorceress's digit....

They fell to squabbling then, Chitra siding with two others against her father, and I left them to debate the Orphic significance of the various dactyls, and which of their prophet's fingers had actually survived its long and savage journey.

The next day, when a band of travelers approached from the south, their dusty robes caught my attention and I left our party to get a closer look at them. Trudging at the head of their column was Shem bar-Yusef, patriarch of the K'Habiru tribe whose lives were spared a year earlier by Droikha's laughing fit. His band were more lean and ragged than ever.

Shem, I said, you're heading the wrong way again. Jebu Ur-Salim lies to the south.

Our god will guide us, he answered, and marched on. Some paces behind, angrily muttering to herself, plodded his wife.

Having no tents, we slept in the open. One night I felt my rug lifted; Chitra slithered in beside me and shucked off her tunic, nipping at my neck with her sharp little teeth.

Chitra, I said, stop. I can do nothing for you about Manu. You're wasting your time.

I don't care, she said. Anyway, we'll see.

To my great shame her touch put me immediately into a helplessly engorged condition, and though mentally I cringed with remorse for this betrayal of Melisanthe, our passion was quickly consummated. A few feet away, Kasperius failed to stifle a snicker. Thus I lost my virginity beneath a dusty Konya carpet on the plains of Mysia, a small and damp but notable point on the great map of my life, a point which I later whimsically graced with a name grander than it perhaps deserved. I could defend my weakness better - after all, I was but sixteen and the girl was uncommonly strong for her size - if I had not, to my even greater shame, allowed her to return the next night, and the next, and again after that.

One such night, after Chitra had gone, Kasperius prodded me back from sleep.

See here, boy, he said, I don't wish to be indelicate, but there are things we must discuss.

What things?

Well, this business with Chitra, for example. Have you been adequately taught the facts of life?

After a moment I caught his meaning.

Oh, yes, I assured him. We know all about that. We use an ointment she concocts, grinds fresh in a mortar - it's absolutely foolproof, she says. It's made from crocodile dung, sour milk and honey.

Crocodile dung? Kasperius peered at me through the darkness for some time. Well, he said, no worries then - that should work just fine!

We moved then through a bleeding land, at times only a week behind Alcibiades and his army, so we were told. The inns, the shops and merchants were stripped by war, and in this wasteland we had to forage for food and water. Camel urine, we found, is bitter but not salty, and has other uses as well: it kills lice, repels sand fleas and straightens hair. Some days we ate nothing but the boiled marrow-bones of slaughtered cattle. Here and there we were threatened by bandits, but our numbers were too great for them and they passed us by. It was, however, within our own company that we might better have looked for danger.

The nightly debates between Polyxo and Kasperius, whose increasingly sour mood seemed aggravated by the jolting of his camel, our poor diet and other miseries of the trail, continued. One evening Polyxo spoke of the soul's journey to mirthless hell, and of how he believed, as did Sokrates, that it was possible for the virtuous man after death to enjoy a happier plane in the ether, nearer the gods if not among them.

Counting yourself, no doubt, in this elite company?

I strive to be worthy of it, said Polyxo.

But see here, Kasperius said. You and I have in common certain beliefs - that rape and torture are pernicious, for example - beliefs which can only be considered virtuous. You derive these from what you claim is Divine Natural Law dictated by the gods, whereas I deny the gods but reach the identical beliefs by logically deducing that they mutually benefit us all, in the form of civilization. We hold the same virtuous positions, yet you think you'll hobnob with Zeus in some jolly, bogus hereafter for giving him the credit for these ideas, while I'll be condemned to gray Hades for having figured them out for myself. Congratulations. You've made a splendid case that critical thinking is evil.

Hubris, said Polyxo. You won't dwell among the gods by insulting or ignoring them. Surely the eternity of death is too important a matter to risk gambling away on those notoriously fallible dice you call critical thinking.

Eternity – feh! Your pathetic greed is appalling, Polyxo. Wine and song and fucking aren't enough, you must live forever, too!

Kasperius turned to me.

Pindar's apt, he said. I'll bet even the boy knows it.

I did: O my soul, do not aspire to immortal life, but exhaust the limits of the possible.

But Timalcus, Polyxo said, mere flesh must be animated. When the flesh fails we must account for the animating force and its attributes.

Even a blind man, said Kasperius, smells smoke when the lamp's extinguished. A puff of hot gas into the night, there's all the ether you're ever going to get. We're no more immortal than a hyacinth or a bog violet. Gladly shall we blossom, and gladly must we fall.

You'll sing a different rhyme in Hades, Kasperius. And why demoralize the boy with this lie of finite, hopeless nothing when he might dream of soaring in bliss with the gods? Why rob his life of dignity and meaning?

Kasperius spat into the fire with exaggerated scorn.

Dream is right, he said. Why must you put your holy spin on all that is human? Your humble piety disgusts me. What draws a man to religion? Desperation, fear, hopelessness. It appeals to everything base and low and ignorant in us. And even if the gods were real, they wouldn't have pigs like us as neighbors. Our only reward from the gods is their bottomless contempt. We suck their divine cocks for favors while their priests cut our purses. Where's the dignity in that?

Polyxo gazed intently at him, then rose without speaking and retreated into the night. In embarrassment I sat listening as Kasperius continued to malign the gods and all who worshipped them. Behind him, dimly lit by the glow of our campfire, Polyxo reappeared, lifting a stout firelog above his head with both hands.

The blow struck Kasperius squarely on top of his skull. At that moment he was speaking of the old Chthonian gods, and his teeth neatly severed the tip of his tongue, which shot into the fire. His eyes misted crimson and he toppled slowly over as the camel boys scrambled among the flames, fighting for the sizzling morsel. Haqim won out and, popping the tidbit into his mouth, strutted away, munching on roast tongue of philosopher.

When I reached Kasperius he was already dead. I wiped blood from his mouth and covered him over. Polyxo, with a look of horror and a strange half-smile on his face, backed away into the darkness. We never saw him again, and supposed he'd thrown himself into the sea, or starved to death, or been eaten by bears.

In the dawn the Dactylists and I dug a grave for Kasperius while the caravan moved on. When we'd finished the hole and went for him, we found a fat crow astride his chest, pecking out his eyes, flicking blood from its black tongue. Chitra's father picked up a stone, but not daring to harm another of Cronus's children, I drove the beast away with shouts and gestures. We laid Kasperius, now both mute and blind, to rest, and mounded the earth over him.

Your name, your honor mark this place, I said. I can build you no grand monument, worthy Kasperius, only a few brush strokes, only what rhumb line and median my map may preserve.

Despite his many diatribes against religion, I invoked the appropriate deities, poured a few drops of oil over his grave, three times called his name and asked the gods to go easy on his soul. If he had one. Then we hurried to catch up to the others.

Gloom descended on our journey. The jaws of war had scoured the plow-lands, and the northwest wind wailing out of Thrace turned the sky black with dust and ashes. Armies had passed through before us. No one knew whose side they were on, nor did it much matter. Near one village we startled a flock of griffon vultures up from a field where they were feasting: every man in town had been staked hand and foot to the earth, their mouths forced open and filled with hot pitch, each screaming a mute black omicron of protest.

We passed through a once thriving market town, now drab and defeated. In the square stood a magnificent chestnut tree, to the bole of which an old woman was tightly bound. She was a witch, the townsfolk said; all their misfortunes were her fault, and they would purge the curse by smashing her witchy bones with the stones they were collecting. But most horrible was her demeanor - blind to her fate, she was laughing and chattering, calling out pleasantries to her friends and neighbors. We made haste, hoping to escape before her laughter turned to screams. Roaming the countryside were bands of refugees, turned savage by famine and war, and we went in fear of them, posting guards at night and keeping our few weapons close at hand.

Our grain was gone. We ate bog violets and swamproot and rationed our water. Only Haqim seemed to thrive: once I overheard him lecturing the other camel boys on what sounded very much like Zeno's Third Paradox of Infinity.

On the forty-ninth day of our journey we crossed the Hermus River into Lydia and camped below Mount Sipylus, just as the spring rains began to fall. In the night a band of hillfolk, armed with scythes and axes and crude spears fell upon us, plundering our baggage for food and driving away our camels and oxen. The members of our caravan scattered into darkness. I found Manu, wounded, and dragged him away from the carnage.

We found refuge in a ravine below the mountain; a few pilgrims and a Persian salt merchant huddled nearby. As the sun rose, I could see that Manu's chest had been jaggedly pierced with a spear thrust. He was dying, and I could do nothing for him but wet his lips with rainwater.

You must take the Prophet to Smyrna, he said.

I cannot stay long in Smyrna, I said. I will find your comrades...

No, he said. It must be you! Only you I trust. Take the Holy Dactyl to its destiny. Swear it!

Then he gave me the finger and died.

Think, Lady Moon, how my love came to be.
Turn, Magic Wheel, and drive my lover home.

Chapter Six

The Mashaiya Convention

ONLY A FEW DAZED OR WOUNDED PILGRIMS remained in the area. Of Manu's band of Dactylists there was no sign, and there was no one to help me with the final rites Manu had described to me.

Among the scattered litter of our campsite, I found a few morsels of bread and dates to sustain me and enough dry tinder and firewood to build a small pyre, upon which I laid Manu's body. By late afternoon the flames curled about him and I found a resting place far enough away to avoid the already familiar scent of burning flesh. Though I feared the return of the marauders, I fell into exhausted sleep.

In the dawn nothing remained but ash and embers and my friend's brittle, blackened bones. I found a heavy stone, and smashed open his skull to set free his soul, lest he wakened to the horror of being reborn as a crow. Whatever words were needed I did not have, so, having performed the rites as best I might, stood gazing down at another melancholy coordinate on my map, another plot of hallowed ground for another murdered friend.

When I reached Smyrna two days later, I had only my tunic, long Scythian boots and a muddy cape beneath which nestled, somewhat the worse for wear, my quivered map. Wrapped in silk inside a pouch beside my heart, just as poor Manu had carried it, hung the Prophet's Holy Dactyl, whose presentation to the Mashaiya Convention I'd sworn a reluctant oath to fulfill.

On the road I had seen other stragglers from our caravan, but the Dactylists were not among them. If they had survived, they would make their way to the city, and if I could find them I knew they would relieve me of their savior's remains and its obligations. Of the army of Alcibiades nothing remained but the bare fields and burned farms left behind them. He had in fact been in Smyrna, whoring and drunk, when his fleet was ruinously defeated at Ephesos. Athens recalled him, planning a speedy trial and execution, but again he slipped away. Some said he was in Syria, others that he and a few loyal regiments had returned to sacking the Thracian ports. Once more I was frustrated. Melisanthe might be anywhere, and so might the one man who could lead me to her.

The population of Smyrna, always a large city, was trebled by pilgrims and holy men and transient tribes and refugees. Every square and agora were filled with their tents and blankets and cookfires, as were all the meadows adjacent to town. They were mostly charitable folk, and I had no trouble finding a meal of virpa or bread and wine.

The Chosen One Convention had been timed to coincide with the tenth year festival of the Most Fruitful High Barley Mother, Mariamne, as the Phrygians anciently called her, but known to us Greeks as Cybele, Lady Mooncow. Her grand temple, one of the Seven Wonders, stood on the acropolis, and her famous oracle was hewn into the stony hillside behind it. Below this complex was a large public square with a theater, a megaron for the assembly, a gymnasium and wrestling school, public baths and fountains, a sundial, water-clock and wind vanes.

Here in the heart of Smyrna, amid the scrubbed and freshly painted, ivy-draped columns and statuary, sat the convention judges, to interview candidates for Anointed One. These hundred scholars and theologians were Greek and Persian, Bactrian, Aegyptus and K'Habiru, philosophers from Rome and Phoenicia and Carthage, dark Arabs and blue-faced Celts, the wisest men of their day.

More than a thousand claimants had already been registered; a thousand more waited. They came in turn before this council, singly or in tribes or cults, bearing handsome scrolls or crudely lettered skins or clay disks of petition, presenting claims and testimonials of wisdom and miracles. Some danced ecstatically, naked and tattooed, glassy eyed with hemp or soma; others wore radiant white silk and exotic plumes and came forth in solemn dignity.

I thought of the meager relic I bore. I had promised Manu I would present it, though I could scarcely argue its theology, as this matter was unknown to me, and I thought I would surely be thrown from the proceedings with much ridicule. But mine, I learned, would not be the only such remnant on display. Though such objects as basilisk bones, unicorn tusks and magnetized sky-stones had been disallowed as non-human, the judges had accepted the skull of a Macedonian shaman said to regularly converse with dead Homer, even, on occasion, transcribing the fabled bard's newest epic. And another cult had submitted a stoneware jar of pickled eels, upon the surface of which an image of the Barley Mother, a local favorite, had miraculously appeared. I saw then that all I needed to avoid making a fool of myself were a fresh tunic and a fancy petition.

On my second day in the city I came upon the shop of a scribe, whose entryway was packed with customers. He put me to work immediately, writing letters and deeds for the locals and petitions to the Chosen One judges for the cultists and pilgrims. Once again my father's tutoring had saved me. I had a job and a place to sleep; in a month I'd have money for clothing and would have prepared, in my spare time, an elegant paean to the Digit Divine, at which time I could fulfill my oath to Manu. The earnings of another month would provision me to continue my search for Melisanthe, wherever that might take me.

In the evenings after my work was done I laid out my lamps and brushes and inks to work on the Dactylic claim of holy merit. I selected a fine piece of creamy vellum and began with much respectful flattery of the judges, moving on to what little I knew of the Prophet's early history. Woefully short of facts and uncertain of what he had actually taught, I fretted many hours over how to present his story in the best light. In the end, as there was no one to contradict me, I was obliged to make most of it up. The wisest words I'd ever heard from Polyxo and Kasperius, neither of whom was in a position to object, now sprang from the mouth - while yet he possessed one - of the Prophet, who I soon depicted as not only effect-ing marvelous cures Manu had never described, but levitating and divining the future as well. I even convinced myself that, considering his horrific journey, the fact that any parcel of him at all made it to Smyrna truly was a miracle. Once underway, my text flowed like a graceful river, my lettering was elegant and bold.

One night as I composed I was disturbed by a scuffling noise beside me. I looked up into the gouged eye-pits of Kasperius, blind as ever Homer was, and promptly fainted.

When I slowly regained my senses, he was hovering anx-iously over me. He spoke my name, which I could just make out, and other words which I could not. His truncated tongue, it seemed, along with his sightless eyes, had accompanied him into whatever plane he presently occupied. That it was Kasperius I doubted not, but his form or condition I could not guess.

I shrank back when he reached to comfort me with a touch; he seemed to sense this, and withdrew.

Kasperius, I said, Are you alive, then? Or dead - a ghost?

Yeth, he said. Dead, truly dead, though strangely I have not taken leave of men, of the world of daylight. Ghost, I suppoth, ith the right word, or phantom. But harmless, I assure you - your friend, ghost or not.

This condition, if I may ask, are you not in some distress? Or pain?

To be dead, you mean? Yeth, the wounds, but not the state itself. I have an awful headache. My cursed tongue plagues me and I'm blind as midnight, keep bumping into things. But it's not all that unpleasant: sometimes I float a bit - I wonder if this is that ether business Polyxo used to babble about.

I asked him if he had, as is sometimes imagined, any special powers - clairvoyance of the blind or portents of the dead.

Not exactly. Not in the way you mean.

We were silent for a time.

Look, boy, he said at last, I know what you're thinking. No one is more surprised than I to find myself ambulatory. I'd have given good odds that no such state was possible, yet here I am. Perhaps, even now, the ferryman comes for me. Perhaps I'm already in Hades - I sense vague presences about me at times. I don't know and I can't explain it.

We talked for a long time, his speech growing easier for me to understand. He was aware of the caravan's fate, and of Manu's, but of Polyxo, who he readily forgave, he knew nothing further.

Poor Polyxo, he said. I pushed him too far. His guilt must have been terrible, and I'm to blame.

I played a part, too, I said. That line from Pindar, I regret it now.

I must go now, Timalcus. If you like, I'll come again.

Of course.

Kasperius began to levitate, his form fading into mist.

By the way, he said, thank you for burying my earthly shell so tenderly, even for the prayers. Though I can't say they helped, they certainly can't have done me any harm.

After that the shade of Kasperius came nearly every night, and began to occasionally appear suddenly beside me in daylight, though he remained visible only to me. But he was not the Kasperius of old - his cynical certainty was now colored by musings about a cosmos which was, he said, rather more mysterious than he'd previously imagined. But when I determined that he no more knew where Melisanthe or Alcibiades were than I did, I began to find him a bit tiresome, and to resent his intrusion on my work.

He soon sensed this and became content to sit quietly nearby and listen to the scratching of my brush. He said he was happy just to be among the living and much preferred my company to that of the used-up dead. Before long I grew accustomed to his presence and to his disfigured face, coming to find it less hideous than oddly comforting.

One night he asked leave to interrupt my writing.

I've been thinking about your quest, he said. You will scarcely believe what I'm about to suggest, but since I can't help you, I think you should consult the oracle of Mariamne. It's the oldest in Asia, you know, and the current sibyl is highly regarded.

You, Kasperius - an oracle? Well, I might just as well if I can afford it. I have no idea which direction to go next, anyway.

When I was satisfied with my petition, I left work one day, put on my new tunic and went to register with the council of judges. They entered my name on a scroll and said I'd be called for examination in three or four days. It was a balmy summer afternoon. I wandered up to the temple and stood admiring it. To my eye it was a hundred times lovelier than the sterile angularity of the Parthenon, for the oriental tastes of the Lydians had made them soften its lines with graceful arches, producing an altogether more feminine and fitting shrine for a goddess.

Behind the temple was a pathway leading up to the oracle, lined with stelae boasting of cures or reciting the testimonials of famous clients. Fees were posted at the entrance: a full consultation would cost me a fat ram, plus the usual coins for libations, a reading and so forth.

It was a busy place with a long waiting list. One of the acolytes gave me a small clay tile bearing a number, which I took with little enthusiasm. Perhaps I could afford the price when my number was posted in the city two or three weeks hence; perhaps not.

I descended the acropolis against a long line of vendors and servants carrying up platters of figs, pomegranates, honeycakes, roast meats and other delicacies for the sybil and her priests. I wished Kasperius were with me so that I might describe for him the luxuries being extorted - as he would once have put it - from needy and desperate people, but the old philosopher thought the climb too difficult for a blind ghost.

With my nightly scribal work at an end, I began strolling the city in the evenings. Often I sought out pilgrims, finding them eager to describe their homelands and journeys. From these interviews my map grew thick and rich with detail, with cities, seas, nations, exotic races, with oases, peaks and far horizons never dreamt of by Herodotus.

Other nights I simply wandered, Kasperius by my side. He rested one ethereal hand on my sleeve, bumping into things but causing little damage as his shadow was only marginally corporeal. One evening we found ourselves in the potters' quarter. It was given over for the duration of the festival to the manufacture and sale of deities, which I described to him.

The babble of voices - Greek, Persian, Arabic and others - surrounded us, prayers of the devout, buyers' haggling, the hucksters' patter.

As we wove our way through the crowd I began to notice three recurring faces, three men who seemed to be following us.

I turned to find them shyly watching me. They looked familiar, and when I spoke to them I recognized them as Bactrian travellers whose gods I'd helped the Scythians steal the previous year in Armenia. Since that day, they said, their tribe had wandered, aimless and dissolute, until they'd come to the fields outside Smyrna. These three had been delegated to enter the god market and acquire new deities, hoping by this to restore purpose and order to their people. They bore me no ill will, they said, and begged my assistance with the difficulties of translation and negotiating, a favor I certainly felt I owed them.

We began to browse, overwhelmed by the vast array of merchandise and much plagued by the godmakers and merchants and their hustling touts. Gods and goddesses of every size and style and price were displayed - fierce, fanged catgods of silver, fat earth mothers carved in stone, heads and busts and statues of every celestial in the Greek pantheon, in every size from twice a man's height to the length of a child's finger, and made of clay and marble, wood, stone, gold and bronze. Attending the deities were Herakles, Orpheus, Perseus and other heroes, and there were banks and rows of more exotic foreign gods: Qudsu, Sutekh, Azizos and Zubin Mehta, of whom I'd heard the Scythian shamans sing. One shop specialized in idols from India, the Orient, Persia and Arabia. Another boasted stacks of crusted mummies, carved Aegyptus amulets and models of the Nilotic gods and their consorts. One stall sold chunks of hemp resin, mushrooms and cakes of black soma for those daring enough to seek their gods face to face. Everywhere hung the smoke of incense and the smell of burning fat and lamb's blood.

A street vendor had all the patron gods and goddesses of the arts spread out on his mat: Ganesha, Thoth, Orpheus and countless others. I passed over Orpheus, as I felt he'd been little help to me, and selected a tiny faience carving of Nabu, Babylonian muse of scribes and copyists. I bought him to carry as my own talisman, my helper in the arts of writing and mapmaking.

A merchant seized my arm, dragging me into his shop. Hesitantly, the others followed.

I'm Hyssam, he said, Hyssam the spoiler they call me! I spoil my customers like grandpa spoils the kids, get it? Your name? Timalcus? Now then, Timalcus you've come to the right place. Just look at these prices! Best selection in Smyrna, on the whole coast for that matter. Who're these fellows? Never mind, I have what they need.

My Bactrian friends looked around in bewilderment. Merchandise was strewn about the shop in such chaotic heaps that Kasperius stumbled over a bust of Dionysus and fell in a Pantheonic tangle of divine arms and torsos. From his perch on Aphrodite's knee, a boy of perhaps five watched me help the ghost to his feet, an act Hyssam pretended not to notice. When my comrades' attention fell upon a gilded head from Phoenicia, Hyssam leapt to their sides and clapped his arm over one's shoulders.

A smart choice, he said. A classic. We call him Enkimdu, but you can name him anything you like, really. Look, he even looks like you! Now, are you folks settled or nomadic? Because if weight is an issue, we have him in hollow, and that saves you shekels, too, right? Or how about Melkarth here? He's

Enkimdu's uncle or something, anyway family. Buy him, get a free altar. The Grand Archon of Smyrna has this model - very popular, can't keep it in stock.

The Bactrians edged away, looking at me helplessly.

Now here's a set you might like, just in from Canaan. Buy this big guy, Ba'al, and I'll throw in Astarte for free!

My clients looked at Ba'al with some interest. They asked me to inquire about his attributes.

He's a strict one, said Hyssam. Straighten a tribe right out. Problems with loose morals, mouthy brats, forget about it. If you want discipline, standards, this is the deity for you. And maintenance couldn't be simpler.

What sacrifices does he require?

Well, children are best, of course. You can use prisoners of war, slaves, but you get better service with kids. He'll do a better job for you that way. Hyssam grabbed the little boy's arm and dangled him before us.

Like this one, he said. My son, Titus.

He tousled the child's hair fondly and released him, miming a throat-slitting gesture with his palm.

The sacrificial knife is good. Or bash their little skulls with a club. We have clubs, knives, altars, cheap. Incantation, pour some wine, nothing to it. Afterward you can always eat 'em. Give Ba'al the chine, some fat, put a little fennel on them, delicious. Keeps them in the family, so to speak.

Don't the parents object?

I recommend drums, said Hyssam. Drums or horns will drown out the wailing.

After conferring with my friends I conveyed their reservations about Ba'al to Hyssam the spoiler.

They're looking for something a bit more...liberal.

One of the Bactrians had wandered away and now stood staring into a dark niche, transfixed by what lay within. We joined him and looked in at a bronze head with cruel, sensuous features, cascading hair, piercing eyes and a hint of truncated horns.

Who's this?

This one doesn't have a name, not one you can say out loud. Trust me, you don't want him.

Why not? My friends seem to like him What does he do? What does he want?

Hyssam showed a sudden reluctance to speak.

I don't know what he wants, he said. I probably wouldn't tell you if I did. I don't think it's allowed.

But you must know something about him, I insisted.

Look, said Hyssam, truth is he's a reject. Two different clans bought him, and they both brought him back. Normally, all sales are final, but he's a bad one. Truth is, I think he's defective. Believe me, you don't want him.

Be still, Kasperius, I said. I can't concentrate with you laughing like that.

In the end, the Bactrians settled on Enkimdu, who turned out to be the Sumerian god of canals, a four-headed Visnu from India, and Wadj Wer, the Mighty Green One, an Aegyptus fertility god. The models they chose were clay but beautifully painted in bright lacquers, and light enough to carry.

Hyssam and I began to haggle.

Now folks, he said, I can sell you these, but you'll be happier in the long run with more substantial models. What will your wives say when you come home with these cheap plaster gods?

I made our final offer and drew my mantle around me as if to leave.

You're twisting my testicles, Hyssam moaned. I'm not making an obol on this deal! Wait here, I'll ask my boss....

He disappeared behind a curtain and returned moments later reeking of wine, whereupon we concluded the sale. My clients wrapped their new deities in their cloaks and we headed for the street, Hyssam on our heels.

You need incense? Unicorn tusks? What about an ark? We have arks!

As we left the shop a new customer entered. I heard him ask Hyssam about the all-inclusive invisible god the K'Habiru were raving about, and then their voices were lost in the babble of the street.

At the edge of the god market I parted company with the grateful Bactrians. Kasperius and I considered the improbable journey of their new deities.

I wonder what the rest of their tribe will make of the exotic assortment of new gods they are now to worship, I said.

They're actually quite fortunate, I think, Kasperius answered. Most people are stuck with the gods they're born with, and generations of their elders have named them and defined their natures. These folks are free, for the most part, to invent for their new gods what qualities they believe will be most useful to them. For example, despite Enkimdu's previous function in Mesopotamia, I doubt the Bactrians will suddenly take a fancy to canal building. And their shamans will not be slow in perceiving freshly issued commandments, which only they, of course, will be able to interpret.

I never saw so many gods. In one place, I mean.

Yes, said Kasperius. There were quite enough for all of us.

When it was time for my appointment with the Chosen One council, I excused myself from work, put on my new tunic and mantle and took the Holy Digit and my petition to the agora. As I mounted the steps of the megaron I was jolted from behind and thrown violently down. I rolled over to find Chitra and her clan standing over me.

Where is the Dactyl? she screeched. Where is Manu? What have you done, infidel?

Policemen appeared, thinking I was being robbed. After I explained, they left me with the Dactylist band.

I recognized Chitra, who now called herself Lakshmi, her father and one or two others, including Haqim, but their number had grown. They now numbered a dozen or more, and Chitra seemed to be their leader.

I stood and brushed myself off before speaking.

Manu was wounded in the attack, I said. I did what I could for him, but Death ate his name. I have as well honored his further wishes.

I placed the Dactyl's pouch in Lakshmi's hands, gave her father the petition and told them the council awaited their appearance. The clan gathered round her and the precious relic, faces bright with awe. Silently they turned away and filed into the assembly hall, leaving the thanks I felt they owed me unsaid. Later in the day I learned that the Digit Divine had been accepted for consideration as Mashaiya, and that the judges' decision was heavily influenced by the beauty and eloquence of the petition which accompanied the Prophet's scant remains.

That night I told Kasperius about it.

Ah, he said. So once again the finger has changed hands. It must have been quite touching.

Yes, yes - very funny.

But don't you see what this points to?

Stop it, Kasperius.

Clearly the judges found it a gripping story. You might even say that it tickled their interest. Now if the digit can just knuckle down and somehow gain a hold in the competition, why then - even the ultimate prize may not be beyond its grasp!

It gave me some cheer to discover that death does not necessarily rob a man of his sense of humor, even if all that remains is a flair for terrible puns.

By the feast of midsummer, examination and registry of the candidates were complete and the judges retired to their deliberations, but not without scandal. One savior's chief patron, a rich sultan from Sardis, boasted too publicly of having bribed several judges. The boast proved true; he and four judges, with their families and retinues, were expelled from the city, driven from the gates and pelted with feces and rotted fruit by angry pilgrims. Thereafter, the proceedings were generally regarded as honest.

The Cybelline festival drew to a close with celebrations and parades throughout Smyrna. Mimes and song-stitchers and jugglers performed; fire-eaters, contortionists and African dwarfs were on display. In every street, prophets and seers preached and cults conducted mystery plays of Pan or Orpheus or the Rites of Eleusis. The city throbbed with drums, ritual and song. Seekers, apostles, gawkers and cutpurses filled the squares.

In the agora crowds lined up to see the Living Goddess, as she was called. When my turn came I saw a pale, malnourished lunatic, moonblind from staring at the heavens. A rambling stream of words poured ceaselessly from her lips - she jabbered worse nonsense than any drug-addled sybil - but the more recondite her muttering became, the more wisdom her admirers perceived in it. Even Kasperius listened to her with some interest.

I have no idea what she's talking about, he said, but I can't say there's nothing to it.

New converts swelled the ranks of the Dactylists, among whom further schisms had occurred. Some, following Manu in identifying the Digit Divine as a middle finger, called themselves Epimedites, or Elders of the Holy Fool's Finger. Another faction, disaffected because only Lakshmi was allowed to handle the Dactyl, had begun chopping off their own fingers, whereupon they would cry out Alleluia, He has replicated!

These Detached Dactylites, as they were known, occasionally engaged in public scuffles with the Orthodox Dactylesiasts, the sect firmly under Lakshmi's leadership and that of her bodyguard, Haqim the former camel boy. Little concern over these incidents was shown by the authorities, since, as tense anticipation mounted over the judges' looming decision, brawls between cults had become commonplace.

A gambling syndicate arose, almost overnight, giving odds and taking wagers on the outcome of the Chosen One competition. Two overwhelming favorites emerged. Siporus, a dapper aristocrat from Rome, held that the gods, given sufficient adoration and gifts, wanted men to be rich and happy. His chief rival was Xorthius of Petra, a gloomy Nabatean patriarch. Life, he taught, was shit and misery, and we might just as well get used to it. Both were enormously popular.

There had been no news of Alcibiades in months. After his neglect had cost the Athenian League most of their warships, they'd withdrawn from Asia Minor to defend the Attic homeland with what forces they had left, ceding the Aegean to Sparta. Lesbos and the other rebel isles were safe for the time being, as was Smyrna and the Lydian coast where I lingered in comfort if not contentment. My employer had come to value my services so highly that he offered me a partnership and the hand of his youngest daughter, and was sad when I told him I must leave Smyrna soon. As my needs were small, I had amassed sufficient funds not only for the continuation of my quest, but enough to buy a ram for the oracle as well. I kept him behind the shop and called him, to tease Kasperius, by the name Polyxo. What I did not have was any idea which way to go when I left Smyrna.

My number was at last posted in the agora, and on the day of my appointment I took sleek, wooly Polyxo up to the shrine of Mariamne's oracle. The priests there were more sophisticated and professional than those at Antissa or Trapezus; they performed the rites of ablution and libation and sacrifice with brisk skill, and we went inside.

In the dim, smoky antron I watched them bring out the famous sibyl, seat her on the tripod and unstop the fuming vent at her feet. She was shockingly obese. Beneath her sheer gown flabby folds hung from her belly and limbs and her puffy cheeks pinched her eyes into narrow, porcine slits. She huffed now and again from the sulfurous vapor but ignored the dish of herbs brought to her, seemingly already drugged into a state of vacant befuddlement.

Ask your benison, said the priest.

Help me, Lady Mooncow, I said. I seek my beloved - her name is Melisanthe of Lesbos.

At my voice the sybil gave a cry as though in pain, arching her spine with a spastic jolt.

Behold! said the priest, Mariamne comes!

She began to speak:

Your skin is a scorched field, a cracked urn; A feast for fox and crow,
More bitter still is the cup you seek to taste;
The flames you bid me kindle consume the flesh of every vessel;
What I know I would throw off like a poisoned cloak;
The cloth you'd have me spin for you demands threads
Not yet dyed to color your tapestry....

At the hexameter's end, attendants moved to help her from the podium, others to usher me out. All of us froze in astonishment when she rose heavily to her feet and continued, her voice rising:

Yet your libations and blood dish compel me further to speak,
To suffer the flash and shimmer of phantom time,
And so convict you of the crime you have not yet committed....

Something about the girl moved me deeply; her voice had a haunting quality, a memory of ancient madness. As the uneasy priests held a whispered consultation, I edged nearer her stage. Her body began to shiver violently. She was overcome with a brief frenzy of laughter, and her last rhymes came in wild shrieks, lacerating the antron's stony echo:

I beg thee! I beg you get thee to the bliss of thy poor fancy;
Be still and leave me to my hell!

Her eyes opened wide in horror, eyes as emerald as the shoals of Lesbos. I rushed toward her.

Melisanthe, I cried. Do you know me?

Priests were beside her, struggling to grasp her flailing hands. She clawed savagely at her face and eyes with sharp fingernails, gouging bloody weals that spattered their scuffling dance. Acolytes scurried about; an upended torch fell hissing to the floor; her wails were no longer human.

Attendants seized me and began to drag me away.

What have you done to her, you wretch?

She collapsed then into the priests' arms and I found myself suddenly flung outside in the dust. A crowd surrounded me.

What did he do?

A priest looked at me in disgust.

He's killed the sibyl, he said. That's what he's done.

Angry patrons and acolytes fell on me, shoving and spitting. I crawled away and climbed sobbing to my feet and staggered off, pelted with stones and curses. Somehow I made it home.

During the three days the beloved sybil lay shuddering and delirious, her extraordinary performance and my alleged role in it were the talk of Smyrna. I dared not go anywhere near the oracle or the great square, but I picked up rumors from our scribal customers. The sibyl, it was widely held, had come to Smyrna as a young whore from Ephesos, a bit too chubby and loquacious for that trade but with an innate talent for oracular rhyme. Before that, some said, she'd been an island girl made captive in the war. But others claimed she was Syrian, perhaps half K'Habiru, and a few insisted she came from a noble Macedonian family, or that she was only a local peasant girl. Thinking that Kasperius might know the truth, I called out to the ether for him, but he did not come.

On the fourth day she died.

The city mourned and the Chosen One judges adjourned for her funeral. Hooded and cloaked, I watched the keening procession from my rooftop as it wound lugubriously through the streets and out the city gates. None of the cortege, I think, cried more wretchedly than I, for mine were the bitter, love-lost tears of Orpheus in defeat. Kasperius appeared then, beside me.

Was it her, Kasperius? Is that why you sent me to the oracle?

He answered slowly and with great tenderness: I believed there was something there you needed to hear.

But was it her? Can there have been another such pair of eyes in this world?

I would tell you if I knew, said Kasperius. But this is not given me. I do not know.

That night I packed my belongings and made my way cautiously from the city, heading north. In the midst of our mourning, fresh news had arrived concerning the swine Alcibiades, and I now had some idea of his hiding place.

Think, Lady Moon, how my love came to be.
Turn, Magic Wheel, and drive my lover home.

Chapter Seven

Alcibiades

ALCIBIADES WAS A HUNTED MAN. Teams of assassins had been dispatched to slay him, one by Athens, another by the Persians and a third by the Spartan general whose wife he'd seduced. One of the rumors circulating suggested that he had given most of his Thracian plunder to Pharnabazus, Basileus of Phrygia, in exchange for refuge in that king's domain. I found this story credible since I knew, from my days in Athens, that Pharnabazus was his wife's godfather. Somewhere in the back country of Phrygia, I believed, in a villa with his current mistress, Alcibiades lived in seclusion and anonymity - a gentleman farmer, a harvester of grape and olive - plotting, no doubt, some fresh villainy against his species.

Kasperius seldom left my side; we made our way back up the coast, through towns and cities being slowly repopulated and mended. By then I was well seasoned in the skills of survival on the road. A year passed. When my money ran out I took work as an assistant scribe or painter of public notices until pen and brush earned me enough to move on, always quietly seeking news of my quarry, ever a spy among the patrons of taverns and marketplaces.

My map grew spidery with the contours of river, coast and plain. In its burgeoning detail I read the past, the mournful coordinates of grief and shame and loss. Here were fixed in ink the graves of Kasperius and Manu and a thousand other nameless pilgrims far from home; here their numberless footprints; here revisit the semened ground where first I sported Chitra; here measure, if I wish, the leagues from Smyrna Gate to Priam's castle. This landscape, like all landscapes, is haunted. Our tears have channeled this land, our blood paints it. Our wanderings stain the earth with sweat and piss and jism, our dreams construct its features, and into the sandy hillsides our hearts and faces, bleeding, have seeped. And in this town, this anonymous port, this war-scarred city, nothing is revealed, so I fold my map and move on.

A second year began. In Pergamum I learned of two brothers who'd been overheard drunkenly threatening the life of Alcibiades for his having dishonored their sister. They had set off into the interior the day before.

I caught up with them at an inn in the next town. They were easy to identify, boozy and quarrelsome bumpkins arguing much too loudly over their plans. A few bowls of wine made them friendly and garrulous. They were going to kill a great man, they confided, gaining fame and vengeance, and confiscate his wealth for their trouble. They knew the name of the town near which he lived - this much they had beaten out of their wayward sister - but were unsure how to reach it. Until I produced my map, they had no reason to take me along, but when they grudgingly named the village, I pointed it out: Thyatira. Though they could read not a word of it, nor follow its intricate lines, nor tell east from north, my map much impressed them, and we agreed to set out together the next morning.

When they were asleep I crept outside and took the road southeast. By midday I was in Thyatira, asking about the local gentry. The townsfolk described an eccentric noble, often dressed in purple, who lived nearby. Yes, he spoke with a lisp, which they felt obliged to comically imitate for me. At dusk I stood in his olive grove, looking up at a large country house surrounded by broad flagstone terraces. Soft light shone from the windows. Inside, a child practiced notes on a panpipe.

Out of the gloom behind me the two brothers materialized, ragged, grinning, already half drunk - improbably, they'd found their way. I tried to reason out some plan with them but they stumbled off, chortling to themselves, in opposite directions. Cursing them, I made my way through the orchards to the foot of a chalky slope below the terraces. There were shouts from above, and I scrambled up.

My unwanted accomplices had torched the house. Flames showed on two sides and the servants ran out in terror, followed by their mistress and her screaming children. Bolts from the brothers' shortbows whizzed in crossfire across the terrace, wounding a nursemaid. From the house, a man emerged, holding a sword and a singed, smoldering cape with which he had attacked the flames.

Come out, you cowards, he shouted. Show yourselves!

I knew the old wardog at once - the voice, the bearing, the face and manner of Alcibiades. He shook his blade at the darkness.

By the time I reached him, he'd been hit twice. A dart lodged in one thigh, another in his ribs, and he sank down on one knee.

I stood over him at last.

Who are you, boy? What busineth have you with me? Leave my house at once or I shall be forthed to thrash you lifeless.

I am Timalcus of Lesbos, I said. I'm going to kill you. I'm going to kill you to hell. I'm going to kill you to wormshit.

Alcibiades had a sullen expression, more exasperation than fear. Enlighten me, he said. What drives you to murder an innocent man in hith own home, before his wife and children? I'll not beg, you know.

Think back, General. The isle of Melos. The beautiful girl you stole from me. Melisanthe was her name.

What, the Melos business again? Ancient history. Some whore, no doubt, one among thousands. Get over it.

Melisanthe was her name, I repeated. Think. Remember.

I reached for my dagger but found I'd lost it scurrying up the hillside.

Who? Never heard of her.

The truth now, Alcibiades, I said. Cronus is your master.

What? Cronuth? Are you mad?

A row of heavy stone water jars stood on the terrace. As I lifted one, I heard Kasperius groan in anguish somewhere behind me in the darkness. Crackling flames rose from the house. I felt their heat on my face as I raised the jug above my head. Alcibiades knelt before me, blackly silhouetted by the fire. Nearby, his mistress and her children wailed.

He let his sword fall from his grip and began working his fingers in the pious configurations of prayer. I stared at him in utter astonishment: the mudras he performed were the same dactylic gestures of the rites of Orpheus, the same signs adopted by Manu and Chitra and the others.

Before you kill me, he said, kindly allow me to finish my devotions.

In hell, I said. Finish your prayers in hell.

I brought the jug down on his skull with all my strength. It was a big jug, and it broke his head. With that, the general toppled over and finished dying.

His mistress crawled to his side, begging for mercy. The two brothers burst onto the terrace with gleeful cries, drawing their knives to cut off his head and penis.

I picked up Alcibiades's sword and drove them back with such fury that they fled the premises.

Take him, I told the woman. Bury him with such honors as you think he may deserve.

By the light of Lady Moon I found and followed the road west, smoke and wailing and the iron smell of blood fading behind me. In a few days I regained the coast and waited for a boat to Lesbos, serene and blue across the straits.

Chapter Eight

The Mapmaker

AT THE PRESENT TIME, my map is considered the most complete in the Greek world, and demand for the copies my apprentices and I make is great enough to earn me a modest living. Someday another man will draw a better one, and from that I derive no sorrow or envy; the fiercely contested border I paint today is tomorrow's forgotten wasteland. I am content to be one chapter in the long history of discovery.

I have come to suspect that the whole notion of boundary, the line between geography and history, for example, perhaps even that between persona and cosmos, is but a fragile myth by which we live lives of imagined categorization. And, too, I sometimes wonder if men's appetite for my work rests upon more than mere accuracy or the magical influence of tiny Nabu, the god I carry where once I bore another fragment of the divine. To claim that my map holds some key to the human riddle or, more than incidentally, the ebb and surge of history, is of course absurd. But look closely: is the isle of Melos formed in ink, or by a single perfect tear of shame? What crimson is it that colors the sands of Lydia? More goes into a map than the casual traveller who consults it may see.

Certain perquisites attach to the cartographer's craft as well. Should a place have no name, or bear one that displeases my ear, who shall object if I bestow upon it something more euphonious to attract the rambling tourist? Caravans now rest, for example, at the Oasis of Lakshmi. And quite near the desolate spot where we buried Kasperius stands a row of squalid huts previously lacking even the status of village. But my own clients may with perfect confidence identify this place as the town of Kasperiatum, though its grand title and the implied history of its etymology baffles them. Thus the landscape speaks; at every juncture a narrative waits.

My parents were alive and well when I returned to Mytilene. Although I felt much changed, Father recognized me at once; he seemed, however, quite unaware that I'd been absent the past four years. They are both frail now - it's doubtful they will survive to see me marry and have children of my own. One day soon Kasperius and I will see them out of this world and into some other, or none at all, a question which the philosopher ghost and I have yet to resolve.

Often, when the windy Lesbian autumn begins and the orchards denude their branches and the dark sea stirs, I am overcome with moods of melancholy which those around me suffer me to endure alone. But of course I am not alone. As I wander the Mytilenian shore, Kasperius walks beside me.

Death has failed to provide him much in the way of magical powers - most of the news from abroad he learns from me. We were sorry to hear about Athens and old Sokrates. Sparta took the city, destroyed her walls and smashed her gods, leaving behind a cruel gang of tyrants to run things. When they were overthrown, the demos, on return to power, blamed Sokrates. He lies now in prison under sentence of death, too stubborn to compromise enough to save his own skin.

Kasperius and I let the sad past lie quiet for the most part, but we have often mused on the outcome at Smyrna. To everyone's surprise, a seemingly ordinary young woman from Libya was elected Chosen One. When she was presented to the public she began to lay out new rules for human conduct thenceforth. War and torture and rape were expressly forbidden, she said, greatly displeasing the politicians and generals in the audience. Rich men were to share with the poor and wealthy states with their starving neighbors. Slavery was abolished. Hissing was heard and scuffles broke out in the crowd. When she said that science and reason were valid forms of truth, and that every man and woman might worship what gods they pleased, or none at all, cries went up:

Heretic! they shouted. Atheist!

By the time she insisted that dark men and yellow ones were not less than white ones and that women were the equal of men, it was no longer possible to hear her. A massive riot erupted and she barely escaped the city alive.

After a few days of deliberation, the judges announced that because the candidate with the second greatest number of votes - Siporus the Optimist - had also fled the violence, the third-place finisher, the Holy Dactyl of the Prophet of Gujarat, Orthodox Branch, was now officially Savior of Mankind. And since the sole requirement of Dactylism, as Lakshmi set it out, was professing the divinity of the Digit, no one raised any objections. People began to worship the Dactyl and, as to the rest of mankind, do just as they had always done. Haqim the camel boy took the new name of Krishna-Ji and became Lakshmi's consort. Together they led a triumphal procession of many thousands of converts back to India.

But the Dactylists, from their beginning, had been predisposed to schism, and Lakshmi's column never arrived in her homeland, having splintered into a dozen factions and subcults along the way. Today, relics solemnly exhibited as the one true original Digit Divine may be seen and venerated in shrines in Punjab, in Persepolis, in Chaldea and Gaul, and other places as well.

So, what was gained, Kasperius? Did the convention accomplish anything of value?

The intent, I suppose, deserves our respect, though a noble failure, if such it was, is still a failure. Pindar would probably have called it an exercise in defining the limits of the possible. Not every story has a meaning. What do you make of it all?

I think much but know little, just as you used to teach, old shadow friend. Not every question we dream up has a solution, it seems, yet we stubbornly demand answers rather than face the horror of not knowing. There are no gods and the oracles are their voices, prophetic tongues so dizzily bewildered by past, present, lies and dreams that teasing out their meaning, which we insist on, is but a mad and futile game. And yet the gods are quite real, thousands of them, as real as we make them, tenderly nurturing one day, cruel and careless the next, mirrors of ourselves in both our sweetest compassion and blackest depravity. We can follow their maps or our own, but the destination remains the same. We're an odd species, Kasperius. We search for things not lost, covet that which is neither attainable nor necessary and pester the heavens we invent for more, always more. A man, given a lifetime, may learn something useful and true. Mankind, never. And so it goes, in all times and all nations, the same and forever the same.

Well, said Kasperius, that's one way to look at it.

Glossary

ALCIBIADES (c. 450-c. 403 BCE): Athenian aristocrat, statesman and military leader (pron. Al-ka-BI-a-deez).

CHTHONIAN, CHTHONIC: Pre-Hellenic deities or spirits living primarily underground.

CITHARODE: Entertainer, amateur to professional, who sang story poems while accompanying himself on a lyre.

COLCHIS: Kingdom on the far eastern shore of the Black Sea; home of the Golden Fleece until Jason and the Argonauts nicked it.

CRONUS (CRONOS, KRONOS): Ancient pre-Hellenic crow-god and titan, father of Zeus and the other Olympian deities, who he ate to prevent them from deposing him.

CYPRIS: Another name for Aphrodite, Greek goddess of love and beauty; the classical Greeks thought she might have originated on Cyprus.

DEMOS: Citizens.

GUSLE; Stringed instrument similar to a zither or mandolin used by Slavic peoples in eastern Europe/western Asia, having a disagreeable, screechy tone; it accompanied the singing of long, tragic hero epics sung in a whiny monotone. There's no evidence the Scythians had gusles, *per se*, but they certainly employed something quite similar.

HOPLITES: Greek heavy infantry.

ILIUM: Troy.

JEBU-UR-SALIM: Ancient name for Jerusalem.

K'HABIRU: Hebrew.

MASHAIYA: Hebrew for "anointed one;" (Greek "Messiah").

PIRAEUS: A few kilometers south of Athens proper, from ancient times to the present the sea-port for that city.

PNUM: Fictitious god created for this narrative.

STADES, STADIA: Plural of "stade," a unit of measurement approximately 600 feet long, being about 9 stades to a modern mile.

STRIGIL: Flat-bladed instrument for scraping the skin clean when bathing.

TROAD: Troy and the area around it, including its smaller vassal towns.